Chloe Gasped. In *Her* Bathhouse, In *Her* Old Enameled Bathtub, Was A Cowboy.

Up to his neck in hot water. And wearing only a hat tilted low over his forehead.

Electric blue eyes met hers and gave her a long, appreciative look.

"Hello, darlin'," he said with a lazy grin. "What can I do for you?"

She swallowed hard. "You can get out of my bathtub."

Obligingly, he braced his hands on the edge of the tub and stood.

She should have closed her eyes.

She should have looked away.

She should have run for her life.

But she didn't. She stood there and stared at the lean, hard body of a magnificent man in all his naked splendor. Her face flamed. Her knees wobbled, and she began to tremble uncontrollably for no reason at all. Except that she'd had a long, hard day.

And it wasn't over yet....

Dear Reader,

MEN! This month Silhouette Desire goes man-crazy with six of the sexiest, heart-stopping hunks ever to come alive on the pages of a romance novel.

Meet May's MAN OF THE MONTH, love-wary secret agent Daniel Lawless, in *The Passionate G-Man*, the first book in Dixie Browning's fabulous new miniseries, THE LAWLESS HEIRS. Metsy Hingle's gallant hero protects an independent lady in danger in the last book of the RIGHT BRIDE, WRONG GROOM series, *The Bodyguard and the Bridesmaid*. Little bitty Joeville, Montana, has more tall, dark and rugged ranchers than any other town west of the Mississippi. And Josh Malone has more sex appeal than all of 'em put together in *Last of the Joeville Lovers*, the third book in Anne Eames's MONTANA MALONES series.

In *The Notorious Groom*, Caroline Cross pairs the baddest boy ever to roam the streets of Kisscount with the town virgin in a steamy marriage of convenience. The hero of Barbara McCauley's *Seduction of the Reluctant Bride* is one purebred Texas cowboy fixin' to do some wife-wranglin'—this new groom isn't about to miss a sultry second of his very own wedding night. Yeehaw! Next, when a suddenly wealthy beauty meets the owner of the ranch next door, he's wearing nothing but a Stetson and a smile in Carol Grace's *The Heiress Inherits a Cowboy*.

Silhouette Desire brings you the kind of irresistible men who make your knees buckle, your stomach flutter, your heart melt…and your fingers turn the page. So enjoy our lineup of spectacular May men!

Regards,

Melissa Senate

Senior Editor
Silhouette Books

CAROL GRACE
THE HEIRESS INHERITS A COWBOY

SILHOUETTE *Desire*®
Published by Silhouette Books
America's Publisher of Contemporary Romance

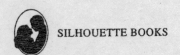

SILHOUETTE BOOKS

ISBN 0-373-76145-7

THE HEIRESS INHERITS A COWBOY

Copyright © 1998 by Carol Culver

Printed in U.S.A.

CAROL GRACE

has always been interested in travel and living abroad. She spent her junior year in college in France and toured the world working on the hospital ship *Hope*. She and her husband spent the first year and a half of their marriage in Iran, where they both taught English. Then, with their toddler daughter, they lived in Algeria for two years.

Carol says that writing is another way of making her life exciting. Her office is her mountaintop home, which overlooks the Pacific Ocean and which she shares with her inventor husband, their daughter, who is now twenty-one years old and a senior in college, and their seventeen-year-old son.

One

The day was hot, the trail was long and her suitcase was so heavy she almost regretted packing her portable espresso machine. But a summer without good coffee? Unthinkable. Especially a summer where the days are warm but the nights are cool. Chloe rested her fanny against a pine tree to catch her breath and unfolded a piece of tattered, yellowed paper that she took from her pocket.

Paradise Hot Springs, where the Ute Indians once wintered near warm thermal waters, invites tourists to enjoy warm days and cool nights in the mountains of Colorado. Mineral waters known to cure gout, obesity, broken hearts and old gunshot wounds. Guests will be met by stagecoach. El. 7500 ft. Your genial host and proprietor: Horatio W. Hudson. Est. April 1912.

"Where is the stagecoach?" she muttered. "And where is the genial host?" She knew the answer to that one. Great-Grandpa Horatio Hudson was dead at age ninety-seven. And Paradise Springs was hers now. If she could find it. There had been one hand-carved wooden sign that pointed the way, and then nothing. Just a narrow trail overgrown with black-berry thorns and nettles.

Nobody told her she'd have to leave her car at the entrance. Nobody told her she'd be walking miles uphill in suede chukka boots.

"Buy boots," they'd said. They didn't say what kind.

"Take your camera." It was hanging around her neck like an albatross.

"Have a great vacation." She sighed. Maybe once she got there.

After another two hours of wading through a shallow creek, spanning fallen trees and climbing at least another thousand feet in altitude, Chloe was dripping with perspiration and gasping for breath. For two cents she would have thrown her suitcase over a cliff, coffeemaker and all.

But then she saw it in the distance. Steam rising in the clear blue sky. With one last burst of energy she dragged herself forward to the end of the trail. And there it was: Paradise Hot Springs in all its glory.

A group of dilapidated log cabins at the edge of a clearing.

A huge, empty pool, cracked and stained with or-ange.

An abandoned wooden bathhouse.

The pungent smell of minerals in the air.

She set her suitcase in the clearing, left her camera on top of it, and walked to the bathhouse. From the looks of the place, this was the end of the road. And the end of her dream.

She pushed and the door swung open on rusty hinges. She gasped. In *her* bathhouse, in *her* old enameled bathtub, was a cowboy. He was up to his neck in hot thermal water, wearing only a hat tilted low over his forehead. Shafts of sunlight poured through the cracks in the roof, illuminating his broad shoulders and large feet. The rest she could only imagine.

He turned his head. Electric blue eyes met hers and gave her a long appreciative look.

"Hello, darlin'," he said with a lazy grin. "What can I do for you?"

She swallowed hard. "You can get out of my bathtub."

Obligingly he braced his hands on the edge of the tub and stood.

She should have closed her eyes.

She should have looked away.

She should have run for her life.

But she didn't. She stood there and stared at the lean, hard body of a magnificent man in all his naked splendor. Her face flamed. Her knees wobbled.

He came to his senses first and planted his hat against his muscular thighs. "Have a seat," he said, waving his other hand in the direction of a wooden bench along the wall.

"Who—who do you think you are?" she sputtered.

"Who do *you* think I am?" he inquired. Tiny drops of water slid down his chest, caught in the damp blond hair there and caused her heart to pound erratically.

"I think you're an intruder and you're trespassing on my property," she said stiffly.

"Your property..." A whole series of emotions— including shock and surprise—crossed his craggy face. But he recovered quickly. "Then you must be..."

"Chloe Hudson."

"Zebulon Bowie," he said extending his hand to grasp hers. "My friends call me Zeb."

"Mr. Bowie," Chloe said, trying to ignore the large callused hand that held hers and didn't let go. "What are you doing here?"

"What does it look like?" he said with a mocking smile.

"It looks like you're taking a bath in my tub, and I would appreciate it if you, if you...if you..." What was wrong with her, allowing the presence of a naked stranger to cause her mind to go blank and her body to hum like a live wire? She was a nurse, for heaven's sake. She'd seen naked bodies before. But not like this one.

"If I would make room for you? No problem," he assured her. "You look like you could use some hot water." Again the frankly sexual gaze raked her body and caused an instant and unwanted reaction. Her nipples peaked against the damp silk shirt that was pasted to her body. "And a cold beer," he added.

"I don't drink beer," she said primly while her

face burned and her parched throat ached for something cool, anything. But accepting a drink would
make it look like he was the host and she was the
guest. And make it all the more difficult to kick him
off her property.

"Too bad," he said, letting her hand go and reaching behind him to grab a pair of clean jeans and a
shirt from a shelf above the tub. "Made it myself.
Won second prize last fall at the county fair."

She exhaled slowly. Her mouth was as dry as a
cotton swab. "Well, maybe just a sip," she said
weakly.

He nodded and brushed past her on his way out
the door, causing her to tremble uncontrollably for
no reason at all. Except that she'd had a long, hard
day. And it wasn't over yet.

Zeb stood in the shade of an evergreen tree and
pulled his jeans on over muscled calves and thighs.
Then a clean, though wrinkled, shirt went over his
damp head of hair. His skin cooled rapidly in the dry
air. But his body was hot and buzzing with awareness.

So this was Chloe Hudson. If he'd known she had
long gorgeous legs that didn't quit, spectacular
breasts clearly outlined by a clingy damp silk shirt,
and a face the angels would envy, he would have...
What? Given up his plan to buy her property and
resell it at a huge profit? Not a chance. Not even if
she'd jumped in that tub with him and he'd watched
the water bead on her smooth skin, traced its path
with his tongue as it trickled down her neck.... What
did she need an old hot-springs resort for? He, on

the other hand, had a desperate need for cash. Now. And no need for sexual gratification. Not from little Miz Hot-Springs Heiress.

He grabbed a cold bottle of beer from under a rock in the stream, then lifted her suitcase and carried it to the bathhouse. "Got your brew for you," he announced. "And your duds."

No answer. He should have warned her about taking care in the hot tub. Some people, unused to a sudden infusion of hot mineral water, fainted dead away. He yanked the door open.

Her head was tilted back against the porcelain, her red-gold hair cascading in wet ringlets over the edge of the tub. Her eyes were closed.

"Chloe!"

Her eyes flew open and she gave him a look that could have shattered the bottle in his hand.

"I knocked," he explained, his eyes riveted on the slope of her smooth shoulders as she sank deeper into the water. But not so deep he couldn't catch a glimpse of rosebud-tipped breasts floating like strawberries in a glass of champagne. He drew in a ragged breath, set the bottle on the floor and walked out.

So now they were even, he thought as he stomped down the rickety steps to solid ground. She'd seen him and he'd seen her. It wasn't as if he'd never seen a naked woman before. Then why was his heart pounding in time to some distant drum?

He glanced back at the bathhouse. "Hey," he yelled. "I left your bag at the door."

No answer. He could go back in. Make sure she hadn't succumbed to heat prostration and didn't need mouth-to-mouth resuscitation. Oh, lord. The idea of plundering her mouth, exploring the moist hot recesses, set his pulse racing.

As he stared at the door, it opened. Slowly, cautiously, she stuck her head out, extended one bare arm and dragged the tan leather bag inside.

Enough, he told himself. Enough ogling his new neighbor and fantasizing about saving her life by holding her flat against the floorboards, forcing her lips open, filling her lungs with air from his, his hand cradled under her head. He let out a deep breath. And practiced what he'd say when she came out.

"Welcome to Paradise," he'd say. Then he'd wait a minute to let the irony sink in. "It's not much to look at, but it's all there is. Not to worry. Being the good neighbor I am, I'll take it off your hands. Right after dinner. Then I'll give you a ride to your car...your bus, whatever. And you can be on your way." He smiled with satisfaction. He shouldn't have to say much more. The run-down buildings, the overgrown weeds spoke louder than any words.

Chloe let the last draught of the smooth dark beer slide down her throat, then rubbed herself dry with a rough towel she found hanging from a peg on the wall. Her skin tingled, and her body throbbed. She closed her eyes and said a prayer that when she opened the door, the cowboy who thought he was God's gift to women would be gone.

But he was far from gone. Instead, he was kneeling over a campfire, sun-bleached blond hair falling over his forehead, coaxing a bundle of dry sticks to burn. She noticed broad shoulders in blue denim and muscled thighs in tight jeans. She sucked in her breath. He had a gorgeous body, in or out of his clothes.

She reminded herself that his gorgeous body was trespassing on her property and stalked purposefully toward him across the clearing.

He looked up through a haze of smoke. His eyes traveled lazily up her legs, lingered on her hips and hovered over her breasts until their eyes finally met. The heat from his gaze combined with the warmth of the fire turned her face red and made her heart pound.

"Do you mind..." she began.

"Not at all," he said pointing to a flat rock where she could sit.

It wasn't easy, considering the hot bath and the bottle of dark beer had made her legs feel like Jell-O, but she continued to stand and glare down at him. "Do you mind," she repeated, "telling me what you're doing here? Besides taking a bath, that is."

"Right now," he said positioning a blackened frying pan on the fire, "I'm making us dinner."

She should have declined, but with only a power bar to sustain her since morning, the sides of her stomach were gnawing at each other. With a sigh she gave in and sat down on the rock opposite the arrogant cowboy who'd taken over her bathhouse, without even apologizing for trespassing.

"Do you have a home?" she asked as she watched him toss fresh fish filets into the smoking pan.

"A home, yes. But no hot spring."

"Wife?" she asked. Where did that come from? Whether he had a wife or not was none of her business.

"No wife," he said slanting a glance in her direction. "You ask a lot of questions."

"Wouldn't *you* ask a lot of questions if you found somebody in your bathtub?"

"Depends on the somebody." He gave her a look that made her heart pound in her ears. It could have been the altitude, the bath or the beer, but it wasn't. It was the way he stared at her, his eyes glittering dangerously.

"First thing I'd ask is how long you staying?" he asked.

She looked around at the ramshackle buildings as twilight fell on the old resort and sighed. "I don't know."

"Disappointed? I don't blame you. Old place is falling apart. Not Horatio's fault, though. He did what he could."

"You knew him?"

"Next-door neighbors. He must have mentioned the Bowie Brothers."

"Wild men who raised hell all over the county?"

"Yep," he said with a cocky grin. "So you've heard of us."

"No," she said. "Just a lucky guess."

His grin faded. He piled a stack of crisply fried fish on a tin plate and handed it to her. "My turn to guess," he drawled. "You live in a city. This place looks pretty primitive to you. You're disappointed. You're thinking, what can I do with it? That's where I come in. I'll take it off your hands. Give you a fair price for it."

She dropped her fork. "What?"

"You thought the resort would be fun, exciting, full of charm. But as you see it's a dump."

She looked around. It *did* look primitive. She *was* disappointed.

"But don't make any hasty decisions," he said. "Take your time and sleep on it." He paused. "Where are you sleeping, by the way?" He leaned back against a sturdy pine tree and studied her. With her smooth skin and fine features she didn't look like the type who'd sleep on the ground. She looked like the type who'd sleep in a big, soft four-poster bed with a bunch of little bitty pillows. Wearing a little short silky thing cut low that revealed the curve of her lush breasts and her long legs.

His gaze dropped to the cotton-knit shirt that hugged her breasts and the soft jeans that caressed her hips and suddenly he was short of breath. His own jeans were uncomfortably tight. Maybe he should have waited with his offer. But he was not only out of breath, he was almost out of time.

"I'm not sure where I'll sleep," she said, glancing around at the rustic buildings. "What about the cabins?"

He shook his head. "Stripped. Empty."

"Where *do* people sleep?" she asked.

"Hammock strung up between the trees. Or sleeping bag on the ground."

Chloe's heart sank. "Is that how people got over gout and obesity and broken hearts, by sleeping on the ground?"

"Is that why you're here, to get over a broken heart?" he asked, his eyes glued to her face.

"I'm here to claim my property," she said, hoping

he couldn't see the crimson flush on her cheeks in the gathering twilight. How could he know about her broken heart, her recent divorce? Was he clairvoyant?

More likely he was just an ordinary cowboy. From the look of the muscles straining against the faded denim of his shirt, he spent his days roping steers and branding bulls. Why would he want to buy an old hot-springs resort? Just so he could have a steamy soak at night in peace? The memory of him rising out of the hot steam, his raw masculinity so blatantly displayed, sucked the air right out of her lungs. And still she wondered. A sexy, good-looking guy appears in her tub, plies her with homemade beer, carries her suitcase, cooks dinner and then offers to buy her property. Why?

"There's something fishy here," she said drawing her knees up to her chest.

He looked pointedly at her plate. "You got that right."

"No, I mean—"

"I know what you mean. You think I'm too good to be true," he said in a smug tone that made her clench her teeth. He leaned back against a tree stump and shoveled a chunk of fish into his mouth. "But this is just Western hospitality. It's the custom. Tradition."

The firelight cast shadows on his angular face. Custom, tradition, hospitality? In her experience men, whether architects or cowboys, usually had ulterior motives for their hospitality.

"What would you do with the place if I sold it to

you?'' she asked casually, tilting her head to one side.

"What are *you* going to do with it?" he countered.

"I don't know," she lied. She'd be damned if she'd have some arrogant cowboy laughing at her plans.

"Neither do I." He dumped a handful of ground coffee into the boiling pot of water and Chloe's mouth fell open in surprise.

"What's that?"

"What does it look like?"

"You can't make coffee like that," she said wrinkling her nose in disgust.

"I just did."

"It'll be awful."

"Wanna bet?"

She stiffened her spine against the rock. "I don't bet."

"Don't drink, don't bet. What *do* you do?"

"None of your business."

"If it's any consolation," he said, "I'm not going to turn the place into a casino." He threw that in to reassure her. Not that it was any of *her* business what he did with the land.

She didn't answer. She was looking at the fire so intently she might have been a million miles away.

Zeb was running out of patience with this woman. If he didn't need the land so badly he'd douse the fire and cut out right now. He was an impatient man. He was sick of waiting. Sick of struggling, of trying to raise champion cattle without a champion bull. So he took chances. So what? So he sometimes bet on things that didn't pay off. This one would. It had to.

He set his cup on a rock, then stood and walked around the fire. Glancing down at Chloe, he planned to say good-night and leave. But he saw her hair had dried into a mass of curls, turned red-gold in the firelight. Her chin was propped on her knees as she stared into the flames, dreamy-eyed.

He had dreams, too. And he wasn't going to let some slick, well-endowed city gal put the kibosh on them. His palm itched to reach down and slide his hand through her hair, wind his fingers through those unruly silky curls. Yank her up by the arms. Make her look him in the eye and admit she had no business here. Then kiss those ripe, red lips until his lust was satisfied and he could put her out of his mind.

Was there ever a woman less suited to outdoor life than this one? Of course, there weren't many who were, which was why he didn't mix ranching with women. When he wanted the company of women instead of cows, he went to town. But it was too late to go to town tonight and he had work to do.

He held his hand out in front of her. "Good night," he said.

Without thinking, Chloe took his hand and let him pull her up to face him. Dusk had settled over the old dilapidated buildings and his angular face was in shadows. The only sound was the hiss of the last of the dry birch wood. His eyes were dangerous pools of darkness—the kind a woman could drown in and never be heard from again. An owl hooted in the distance and she gave an involuntary shiver.

"Are there many...uh, animals around here?" she asked.

"Not many," he said. "Just a few bobcats, mountain lions, coyotes...." He braced his hands under her elbows. "You're not afraid, are you?"

"Of course not. I just wondered...what to expect." Her voice shook just slightly as his hands moved up her arms to cup her shoulders, sending tremors up and down her spine.

"Expect the unexpected," he warned. Then he leaned forward and took her mouth with the fierceness of the wild animals she feared. Wood smoke and the heady masculine scent of Zeb Bowie swirled around her. She could have pushed him away. She could have turned and run. Instead, she grabbed a fistful of his cotton shirt and held on for dear life.

He parted her lips with his tongue and she let him in. Met him half way in a duel no one could win— or lose. She wasn't thinking. She was sinking into a whirlpool of passion. For the first time in months, she let all rational thought go—and good riddance.

For the first time in months, years, she felt the heat of passion surging through her veins. The pounding of her heart matched his. He made her feel sexy, desirable, light-headed, lighthearted—and scared. Scared to death of making another disastrous mistake.

She pulled back, breathing hard and pressed her hand against his chest to steady herself. Then she jerked her hand away as if she'd been burned. What was wrong with her, letting some stranger trip all the emotional switches she'd carefully turned off? Hadn't she learned anything in this horrible past year?

"What was that?" she demanded, pressing her

palms together. "Another example of Western hospitality?"

His teeth flashed white like a wolf's in the semi-darkness. He was laughing at her. Thinking she was a greenhorn who'd fall for the first real honest-to-God cowboy who happened along. He didn't know she would never fall for anyone again. Never be taken for a ride again. And never be used.

For a long moment he held her mesmerized with the strength of his gaze. Then he grabbed a bucket, poured water on the fire and fastened his knife to his belt. "You'll be all right?" he asked.

"Sure," she said. She had to bite her lip to keep from screaming, *Help. Don't leave. I'm scared of the dark, the wild animals and being alone.*

"Got your sleeping bag, gas lantern, food in that suitcase of yours?"

Yeah, and a laptop computer and a portable TV. She wrapped her arms across her waist as if to ward off the dangers of the night. "Don't worry about me," she said, certain he was the type who only worried about himself. "I'll be fine."

"Good enough," he said, clamping his wide-brimmed hat on his head. "See ya."

She watched him amble off through the trees, whistling to himself as if he didn't have a care in the world. He didn't know or really care that she had none of the things he'd mentioned. Except food. She had packets of freeze-dried food, but she'd thought…she'd expected…

She had *not* expected a naked cowboy with shoulders from here to there. She had not expected him to feed her or give her a kiss that left her shaken and throbbing with unfulfilled desire.

She staggered back to the bathhouse on rubbery legs, opened her suitcase by the light of a tiny flashlight she carried in her purse, and dragged out a sweater and jeans. She layered them over her shorts and shirt, then considered her options. Every bone ached, every muscle screamed out for a soft bed. But there was no soft bed. There was only a hard bathtub.

After draining and drying the tub, Chloe padded the tub with more clothes from her suitcase, then took a deep breath and climbed in it for the second time that day. With her head resting against the cold, hard porcelain, she stared up at the star-studded sky through the gaps in the roof.

If she could get some sleep then tomorrow she would be prepared for Zebulon Bowie. She would not let him interrupt her, destroy her equilibrium, or make her feel inadequate. Or kiss her. She sat up straight in her makeshift bed and stared into the darkness. What if she was prepared, but he didn't show up? What if she never saw him again? For some reason the thought scared her more than the coyotes and mountain lions put together.

Two

The telephone rang at seven the next morning, jarring Zeb out of a dream. A dream in which he and the beautiful hot-springs heiress threw their clothes to the four winds and raced each other to the bathhouse to make passionate love in the hot tub. But when the phone rang, Zeb realized it was just a dream. He groaned into his pillow and cursed the person on the other end of the line.

His whole body went rigid at the memory of Chloe's luscious body floating naked in the tub. That was not a dream. It was real. *She* was real—maddeningly real. He reached for the phone.

"I found one," his brother said.

"'Bout time. You've been on the road long enough. What's he like?"

"Short neck, broad-chested roan. Eager grazer."

Zeb tossed the blanket off the bed and sat up straight. "What about breeding?"

"Raring to go, they say."

"How much?"

"Negotiable."

"Then negotiate," Zeb ordered.

"I thought we didn't have any money."

"We'll get it."

"Any word from the woman?" his brother asked.

"As a matter of fact—" Zeb ran one hand through his hair until it stood straight up "—she stumbled on to the property yesterday in her high-heeled suede boots, silk shirt and a camera around her neck."

"What'd she say?" Sam asked.

"She ordered me out of her bathtub."

"Not an auspicious beginning," his brother noted. "Did she agree to sell?"

"Not yet. But after a night on the ground without a sleeping bag I reckon she'll be ready to sign over the deed today."

"You let her sleep on the ground?" Sam asked.

A twinge of conscience hit Zeb between the ribs. Was he going to let his little brother lecture him on how to treat a woman? "What was I supposed to do, invite her to use the spare room? Give her Granny's nightgown and kiss her good-night? You want a stranger to make money off Horatio's property instead of us?" he demanded.

"Hell, no. You think I like worrying about foreclosure? But..."

"But nothing. We've got to convince her to sell. Now. Today. Before she finds out."

"Okay, okay. What's she look like?"

"I didn't notice," he lied. Didn't notice her eyes were like brown velvet, her hair a ribbon of shiny copper. "All I know is that she looks like she doesn't belong here. Like a hothouse flower in an onion patch. Anyway I'm heading down there right now to make her an offer. After she's seen the place in broad daylight the answer has gotta be yes."

"While she's sore and aching from a night on the ground. Good plan."

"I thought so."

"On the other hand, is it fair to take advantage of her like that?" his brother asked.

"Is it fair that our herd got hit with the anthrax epidemic and we lost our prize bull? Is it fair that the price of hay went up and the price of cattle went down? Life's not fair, Sam."

"I know that. You know that. But does she know that? What if she quit her job to come out here? What if she has cash-flow problems as big as ours?"

"Nobody's got problems like ours. Anyway, I'm offering her a decent price for the property. She goes home with money in her pocket, and you and I make a bundle on the resale. We buy that bull and we're back in business."

"I've been thinking about the woman."

"*You've* been thinking about her? Don't. Think about cattle. That's what I do." Except in the early hours of morning. Then the face that invaded his dreams was not that of a fifteen-hundred-pound bovine. It was *her* face.

"Ask her what she does. Make sure she didn't quit her job to come out here. Otherwise…"

"Otherwise what, you won't go along with it?"

Zeb asked incredulously. Was this the same guy who ruthlessly cleaned out his friends at poker on Friday nights and never felt a pang of remorse?

"I couldn't, and neither could you, tough guy."

"All right, if it'll make you feel better. But I know she's got a job."

"What is it?"

"I don't *know* what it is," he said, exasperated. "Maybe she's a lawyer or maybe she's a waitress in a topless bar." He didn't mean to raise his voice, but the sun was rising from behind the purple mountains and valuable time was passing.

"Now we're getting someplace," his brother said. "What makes you think she's a topless waitress?"

"I don't," Zeb said. "It's just an idea." But the image of Chloe topless in a tight little miniskirt, with her beautiful breasts bared, sent a shaft of desire rocketing strait to his groin. Now, at seven-twenty in the morning, for God's sake. "I don't know why we're discussing this. We have a plan."

"That was when she was just a name on a piece of paper. I didn't know she was gonna come out here. Now she's a real woman with hopes and dreams."

"You're getting carried away. I asked her what she was going to do with the property and she said *she didn't know.* Does that sound like a woman with hopes and dreams? This is not some helpless field mouse like the ones you used to rescue from the claws of the cat. This is a grown-up woman who's come out here on a whim. Who didn't realize hot-springs resorts went out in the twenties and aren't going to come back."

"Just find out if she's okay with this. If she's got a life."

"And a job. Yeah, I know. But I can't find out anything if I don't get down there."

"So get. We on for Friday?"

"Far as I know."

"I'll be there at six. If my car doesn't break down. It's giving me trouble. Next time I go on the road—"

"You'll have a new car. We'll be in fat city."

Zeb hung up, yanked his jeans on and hoped his brother wouldn't be back in time to catch a glimpse of the city woman. It was just possible she'd appeal to his soft heart and he'd blurt out the truth about the property. Zeb put his checkbook in his pocket and rode his horse down the hill to Paradise Hot Springs.

She was trying to get a fire going. He'd give her points for that. She was bent over a pile of smoldering twigs and all he could see was her firm, round bottom, wrapped in snug blue jeans like a second skin. The throbbing in his groin started again. He cleared his throat. "Good morning."

Startled, she jumped, turned and faced him. Her face was smudged with smoke, her hair was a tangle of curls. There were circles under her eyes. An unwanted pang of sympathy struck him between the shoulder blades.

"Sleep well?" he asked, stiffening his resolve.

"Just fine. I was going to make breakfast."

"What are you having?" he asked.

She watched as the fire flickered and went out. Her shoulders slumped. "A power bar," she said without moving.

"Sounds good."

She reached into her pocket and broke the bar in half. "Here," she said holding out her hand. "I owe you."

"Thanks." He took the square of oats and nuts, crammed it in his mouth and chewed. Did she have to look so pathetic this morning, just when he was ready to con her out of her inheritance? Did she have to share her meager breakfast with him and make him feel like a bastard?

He hardened his heart and slapped his hands together. "Now that we've got breakfast out of the way... Feel like talking?"

"I was going to walk around." Gingerly, carefully, Chloe stretched, then winced as the pain traveled down her spine and lodged in her hip. She was glad he didn't ask where she'd slept. She wanted this rough, tough cowboy to think she'd slept out under the trees on the hard ground. Though how anything could be harder than a porcelain bathtub, she didn't know.

"I'll come with you," he said. "We can walk and talk."

She slanted a look in his direction. What was he doing here, the all-American cowboy in his chambray shirt and low-slung jeans? So damnably comfortable and at ease, as if he belonged here and she didn't. Oozing with vitality and sexy good looks that ought to be outlawed this early in the morning. A decent night's sleep hadn't hurt him one bit. Just rumpled his hair.

She shivered in the early-morning air. Longing for a cup of good, hot coffee, a jolt of caffeine to get her through the morning, she was almost desperate enough. She took a deep breath and swallowed her pride.

"I don't suppose you have any of that coffee left," she said.

"*My* coffee?" he demanded with an amused glint in his eye. "Nope. Sorry. But I *can* offer you a guided tour of the property."

"Don't you have things to do?" she asked. "I thought ranchers were always out branding cattle or, or..."

"Wrestling steers? I did all that yesterday. So today I'm free to show you around. Have you seen the inside of the cabins?"

"No, but you said they'd been stripped. I'd rather see the nice parts." She wanted to see something that would encourage her, something to give her hope that her plans were possible.

"Sweetheart, these *are* the nice parts."

She swept her gaze over the rusty, drained pool, the peeling paint on the cabins and the bathhouse leaning at a rakish angle on its foundations and she felt like crying. Then she thought of her great-grandfather, pioneering out here in the wilderness, building this place from scratch. "There are supposed to be forty acres. I want to see the other thirty-nine," she said firmly.

"All forty acres? Whatever you say. We'll take my horse, Jenny."

His horse whinnied loudly and pawed the ground as if she'd understood.

A cold shiver of fear crept up Chloe's spine. The horse looked enormous, with hooves that could crush a rider should she fall or be thrown off. "I don't ride," she said.

"Don't ride," he repeated, dumbfounded. "Where did you say you were from?"

"San Francisco."

"They don't have horses there?"

"Sure, in Golden Gate Park. You can rent a horse for an hour. It's expensive."

"Here we own them. Here you can't get around without riding. I ride, you don't. So why don't you sell the place to me?"

Chloe put her hands on her hips and surveyed him through narrowed eyes. "Why do you want it so badly? Is there gold buried under the ground? Valuable Indian relics? What?"

He shook his head. "Not that I know of. But come and see for yourself. Don't worry, I'll hold on to you." He grabbed her hand and dragged her to the wild, fire-breathing animal he called Jenny. She stumbled and her breath came in short gasps as she stared up at the beast.

"You're not afraid, are you?" he asked, still holding her hand. "Men have been riding horses for five thousand years. Women, too. Joan of Arc rode a horse."

"Good for her," she said biting her lip. "It's those teeth," she muttered, hardly aware she was digging her nails into his hand

"Jenny's not going to eat you. No offense, but she'd rather have a bucket of hay or oats." His eyes gleamed with amusement. He was laughing at her fears.

She was just going to ask why they needed those

huge powerful teeth if all they ate was hay when Zeb abruptly lifted Chloe by the elbows and turned her toward the horse.

"Left foot through the stirrup," he ordered. "Now swing into the saddle." With one large hand molded to her bottom, he shoved her up and placed her left foot into the stirrup. As she swung her right leg over the horse, she hit its side with her knee. Jenny shook her head and reared up on her hind legs.

Panicked, Chloe fell back against Zeb and knocked him backwards. They staggered across the dirt together until he dug his heels in and wrapped his arms around her so tightly she couldn't move. The seductive scent of her hair and her skin filled his senses. With her back wedged against his chest, his arms under her breasts, she fit perfectly, as if she belonged there. But she didn't. She belonged in San Francisco.

"I can't do it," she said, panting loudly, rubbing damp palms against the sides of her blue jeans.

"Yes, you can," Zeb insisted through clenched teeth. "If you don't get on the horse, then you won't see the rest of the property. And if you don't see it, you'll think I'm trying to hide something from you."

Quickly, so she wouldn't have another chance to protest, he unwrapped his arms and pushed her back toward the horse. "Okay, old girl, calm down," he said. "There's nothing to be afraid of. I got somebody I want you to meet. Reminds me of you. High spirits, long legs, big feet, well-bred..."

"Are you talking to me or your horse?" Chloe demanded twisting her head in Zeb's direction.

"Her," he answered tightening his grip on her

shoulders. "This time give her a minute to get used to you. Let her sniff you. She's easily frightened of strange objects."

"*She's* easily frightened? What about me?"

"That's what I mean. You have a lot in common." He put one hand on the horse's flank, the other he kept clamped on Chloe's shoulder.

"I guess that's a compliment."

"Damn right. This time, swing your leg *high* above her. Grab the front of the saddle and hang on." Before she could protest, he put his hands on her hips and lifted her up. Cupping her round firm bottom with his palms, he paused to consider how fit and trim she was. Probably got that way at her health club. She sure didn't stay in shape by climbing mountains or riding horses.

She landed with a resounding smack into the saddle. Zeb mounted and swung into the saddle right behind her.

He ran his hands down her arms, feeling her muscles tense under his hands. "Relax," he told her. "Back erect." With one finger he drew a straight line down the middle of her back. His hand lingered along the warmth of her backside. She gave a little shiver and sat up straight.

"Very good," he said. She leaned back against him, her seductive rear nestled against his crotch, causing an arousal of unexpected strength. Damn. She noticed, he thought as she scooted forward and looked down at the ground. And gulped.

"What's wrong now?" he asked.

"I'm afraid of heights."

He snorted. "What in the hell did you come to the mountains for if you're afraid of heights?"

"Because they're here. Because this is mine. Because...because..." Her voice quavered.

"Never mind." Zeb put his arms around Chloe to grasp the reins, *not* as an excuse to touch her smooth skin, or graze the swell of her breasts with his hands. Those were fringe benefits. His horse moved briskly forward. "Look straight ahead," he told Chloe. "If you keep your heels down and head up, you won't fall off."

"Is that a promise?"

"I swear on my mother's grave."

"Is...I'm sorry...about your mother."

"Don't be. She's alive and well in Tucson. But she's gonna be buried here."

Chloe shook her head and her red-gold curls brushed his cheek and enveloped him in her fragrance. What was it, lavender, lilac? While he fought the urge to lift the hair from her nape and nibble the soft skin behind her ears, Jenny turned up the hill to the old orchard. Not a bad place to start. A grove of gnarled old fruit trees that hadn't produced for years.

"This is your inheritance," he said, waving his hand at the trees. "There are the hot springs and the cold springs. There's this orchard. And a meadow. And that's it. It's not livable. Especially not for someone like you." Once she realized that, she'd give in. She had to.

"Ooh," Chloe exclaimed as a flock of orioles and waxwings sailed out of the bare branches. "It's a bird sanctuary." As the horse meandered through the apple trees, she sniffed the few fragrant blossoms still lying beneath the trees. "Are these really mine?"

"They're yours, but they don't bear much fruit," he warned. "Haven't been pruned for years."

"But if they were pruned..." she mused as the birds chirped and sang overhead.

He shouldn't have let her see the orchard. Hear the birds. Feel the sun on her face. How was he to know she'd find beauty in a group of stunted trees and a flock of noisy birds? He tightened his legs around Jenny's sides and pulled on the reins with his right hand. It was time to stop being so damned nice. Time to show her the *real* Paradise Springs.

The sun turned hot as they plowed through knee-high brush. Low-hanging branches from spruce trees tore at their clothes. She ducked and drew a ragged breath. This was more like it. Sheep Mountain loomed in the distance. Snow-capped, forbidding, at twelve-thousand feet.

"Most of your property is like this," he explained.

"Where are the cold springs and the meadow?"

"I thought you wanted to see the gold mines and the Indian relics."

Holding onto the saddle with both hands, she turned to look at him over her shoulder. "There isn't any gold, is there?"

"Doubtful. But there are a few arrowheads. If you're willing to dig for them. We'll stop along the creek and you can try the water from the spring. Old Horatio claimed it kept him young and...vigorous."

"Did he ever have it tested?" she asked.

"Not officially. But it worked on him. When he went to town women flocked all over him."

"Oh, *that* kind of vigorous." A flush spread up the back of her neck.

"What other kind is there?" he asked grinning to himself. Embarrassing Chloe Hudson was almost as much fun as kissing her. Almost, but not quite. Next to a slate-gray rocky outcropping he reined Jenny in and jumped down. He held out his arms and Chloe, her cheeks still flushed, lifted her leg over the horse and slid into his arms.

She ignored his question, but she couldn't ignore the man, holding her so close she could feel the heat from his body transfer to hers. As if she hadn't been aware of his body for the last hour. She'd thought getting off the horse would provide a respite, a break from his teasing and innuendoes, from his lusty nature. But now his eyes blazed with desire so hot she couldn't look away.

He lowered his head. His lips were just a breath away from hers. She needed him to kiss her. To prove the first time was a fluke. To show her he was nothing but an oversexed cowboy, a flirt who wanted to buy her property for some secret reason. The breeze rushed through the trees. The sound of a spring bubbled in the distance. She held her breath. She knew what was going to happen. She waited for it, wanted it. Now.

He told himself not to touch her. But after an hour of sitting behind her, her bottom pressed into his rigid masculinity, tendrils of silky hair teasing his face, his resistance was close to zero. He was hot, he was frustrated and he was annoyed that she wouldn't give up and go home.

The longer he waited, the more the tension grew,

like fence wire stretched between two posts. He pressed one hand against her arched back and urged her tightly against him, amazed once again at how well she fit. And then he claimed her with a kiss.

One hot, breathless, soul-searching kiss that left Chloe shaking to the tips of her suede boots. And then another kiss, deeper, longer, stronger. His lips were rough against hers. He tasted like coffee and he smelled like leather. This man she scarcely knew had kissed her again like she'd never been kissed before. Twice. No, three times. And she'd kissed him back. Hungry for the taste of him. Unable to get enough of him. Desire flowed through her veins, thick and hot and heavy. She sifted her fingers through his sun-bleached hair.

His tongue stroked her lips, then plunged in, and she welcomed him. But somewhere she knew it was wrong. Last night could be excused as an experiment, a test. But today...today was something else. She knew he couldn't be trusted, but right now she didn't care. Her hunger, her vertigo, her aching muscles were all forgotten in the ecstasy of a stranger's kiss. From deep in her throat a moan escaped. He answered with one of his own. And brought her closer to him. So close she could feel the heat from his body scorch right through her clothes, and the strength of his arousal press against her belly.

Suddenly dry leaves crackled loudly in the clear air, and the sound of hooves thumped against the ground like hammer blows, sending Chloe flying out of Zeb's arms.

"What was that?" she demanded, her eyes wide with fright.

He shrugged, apparently unaffected by the kisses she found earth-shattering. "Just an elk," he said. "And you scared him away. Don't tell me you'd begrudge him a drink of springwater? Your average male elk has a harem of a dozen females. He needs all the vigor he can get to keep them satisfied."

She folded her arms across her waist and studied him. This outstanding specimen of a cowboy with his broad shoulders, narrow hips and rugged face probably had at least a dozen women to satisfy himself, if his raging libido and hot, steamy kisses were any indication. She had no intention of becoming number thirteen, no matter how deliciously desirable he made her feel.

"Is it my imagination or are you slightly obsessed with sex?" she asked.

"You call it sex, I call it nature," he explained.

"Oh, really? Well, I'd love to hear more about elk and their mating habits, but I feel a little funny," she said pressing her fingers against her temples. Funny was putting it mildly. She was feeling positively giddy. But was it the altitude, or hunger—or was it him? She didn't want to know. She had to get away from him. Think things over. "I think I'll go home," she said.

Relief rushed through his veins. He repressed an ear-to-ear smile. "Sure?"

"Yes, I'm hungry. I'm going to try to build another fire. And heat up some of my freeze-dried food for lunch."

"And then you're going…" He waited, holding his breath.

"Then I'm going to town to get some supplies."

"I thought you were going home."

"Yes, home. To the resort, the cabins, the bathhouse. I can't go home, *home* yet, I just got here."

He ground his teeth. He could have sworn she said she was going home. She couldn't go to town. She might hear something. He couldn't afford to have idle gossip spoil the whole plan. "I'm going to town. I'll get whatever you need."

"I want to see it."

"There's nothing to see," he said.

"There must be something."

"A store. A bar. A bank. Houses. People don't see many tourists, so you'd likely be treated with suspicion."

"I'll explain I'm not a tourist."

"That's just the kind of thing that makes them suspicious."

"But…"

"All right, I'll take you." The idea of her walking around telling people who she was and why she was there made his skin crawl. If he went with her, he'd follow her around, stifle any conversation, filter any news, censor any talk.

"I have my car," she insisted. Damn, she was stubborn.

"That's a three-mile walk to your car. A hundred-yard walk to my place, where I've got my truck parked."

"I don't want to trouble you. You've already done so much for me."

Whatever he'd done, it wasn't the right thing. If he had, she'd be packing up right now instead of talking about laying in supplies.

"I'll make a fire for you. Then I'll drive you to town," he said.

"If you insist."

He insisted. His whole future was on the line. The future of the Bar Z Ranch. And it all hung on her. This woman who was a disastrous combination of stubborn determination, a gorgeous body and a complete inability to take care of herself out here. It was just a matter of time before she said she was going home and *meant* it. All he had to do was wait her out—and keep his hands off of her. It should be no problem. But when he lifted her back on the horse, this time behind him, he realized the change in position had only made things worse.

Her breasts cushioned his back, sending tremors of lust rocketing through his body. Her breath was warm on the back of his neck, her hands laced across his chest, causing him to picture those slender fingers caressing his bare skin. He had to get rid of her. Now. Today. But how?

Three

"**Y**ou didn't quit your job or anything to come out here, did you?" Zeb asked casually that afternoon as they bounced along the rutted road toward the highway in his truck.

"No. Why?"

"The obvious reasons. You might not like it here. It's lacking in creature comforts. There's no way to earn a living. If that's a concern."

"Yes, it's a concern. I'm not independently wealthy. Although…"

He turned his head to look at her. "Although what?"

She pressed her lips together to keep from blurting out that she had a settlement from the divorce. It was none of his business. "Nothing."

They rode in silence until they hit the highway,

then turned south toward the small town of Powder-keg.

"There must be some way to make a living out here," she said watching the rugged landscape pass by.

"I'm starting to wonder," he muttered.

"But you do...make a living."

"Yeah, sure. But it ain't easy."

"I'm not looking for something easy."

"What are you looking for?"

"Something different."

"From what?"

"From what I was doing."

He lifted his hands off the steering wheel in an impatient gesture. "Which was?"

"I'm a nurse."

He gave her a long, searching look she tried to ignore. But the heat from his gaze made her quiver with awareness. The lunch break had not done the trick. One look from those brilliant blue eyes and she was as light-headed as before. Her skin burned and she shivered deep inside. His eyes scorched a trail from her French-braided hair to her leather sandals, lingering on her breasts under her clean, wrinkled T-shirt. She could imagine his broad callused hands touching her there and there and...there.

She shifted to face the side window as her nipples stiffened under his appraisal. What was the matter with her anyway, allowing a stranger to affect her this way? Just because the shrewd eyes that undressed her were the color of the Colorado sky and his face a reflection of every cowboy she'd ever seen in every movie, starting with Clint Eastwood and moving right up to Brad Pitt.

"You don't look like a nurse," he remarked at last.

"Did you expect a white uniform and a starched hat? I'm off duty."

"For how long?"

"Until fall."

He exhaled loudly. "You're staying till fall?"

"That was the plan. Unless..."

"Unless you get bored. There's not much to do around here."

"There's plenty to do at the Springs. It needs a lot of work."

"Unless you sell it to me."

"Why do you want it?" she asked.

"Call me land-hungry. I just want it."

"So do I."

"Why?"

"I can't tell you. You'll laugh."

"No I won't. I swear."

"Is this it?" she said as they came to a sign reading Welcome to Powderkeg by the side of the road.

"Don't blink or you'll miss it," he warned.

A row of restored two-story buildings lined the main street. Beyond them, lush green fields stretched out in every direction toward the mountains. It was as peaceful a scene as she'd seen in any Western movie. She opened her window and drew a deep appreciative breath.

"I thought you said it was nothing," she said. "I'll bet it hasn't changed since the stagecoach came through on its way to Paradise Springs. The women will love it.''

"The women?" he asked, startled.

"Or the men. Men are welcome."

"I'm glad to hear it. Otherwise I'd have to slap you with an antidiscriminatory suit."

"Against your next-door neighbor?"

"I don't need another neighbor," he muttered, as he parked in front of the dry-goods store. "I need the land."

Chloe shot him a swift look. His eyes were as hard as flint. His mouth set in a grim determined line. Had he said what she thought he'd said? She shook her head to clear it as she opened the door and jumped down from the front seat of the truck. He didn't want her there. But he wanted her land. What would he do to get the land? What *wouldn't* he do?

Zeb sat in his truck and watched her walk away, forgetting his vow to stick by and stand as a buffer between her and the town and the gossip. He had a sinking feeling that the land was slipping away from him. The land and the deal and the money and finally his own land. It was all her fault. Whatever plans she had for that property, they were completely unrealistic and ill-conceived. Why couldn't she see that?

He got out of the truck and in a few brisk strides caught up with her inside the store. She was looking at sleeping bags. While he leaned against the counter, surveying her through narrowed, disapproving eyes, she bought one sleeping bag. Then a gas lantern and a hammock. A camping stove. The higher the bill she racked up, the lower his spirits sank. She looked at him across racks of anoraks and khaki shorts.

"What else?" she asked him.

The saleswoman turned around. "Zeb! I didn't see you. I should have known," she said with a wink. "New girl in town. Zeb Bowie's not far behind."

"Actually she's not new, Wilma. She arrived yesterday."

"Where you staying?" Wilma asked Chloe.

"At Paradise Springs."

Wilma dropped the calculator she was using to total Chloe's purchases. "But the place is a shambles. Horatio let it go downhill, the old devil."

"I'm thinking of restoring it," Chloe said.

"But haven't you heard…"

"She's heard all about old Horatio," Zeb interrupted. "She's his great-granddaughter."

"No kidding?" Wilma tilted her head to one side. "Now that you mention it, I see the family resemblance. Don't you, Zeb?"

Zeb let his gaze travel up and down her body once again. His pulse accelerated as he remembered how she'd looked in the bathtub, her skin wet and warm and satin-smooth. Her face flushed under his scrutiny. Maybe she remembered the moment, too, when he stumbled in to see if she'd succumbed to the therapeutic waters.

"Now I see it," Zeb acknowledged, snapping out of his reverie. "It's the grizzled grin. And the bowed legs."

Wilma cast a quick glance in the direction of Chloe's shapely legs. "Don't pay any attention to him…Miz…."

"Hudson," she said. "Chloe Hudson."

"Pleased to meet you."

"Why don't you throw in an inflatable air mattress," Zeb suggested. Then he bit his tongue. What was wrong with him, making helpful suggestions? He wanted her to be so stiff and sore from sleeping on the ground, she'd be gone by tomorrow.

Chloe nodded and Wilma went to the back room to look.

"She doesn't seem the least bit suspicious," Chloe whispered.

"That's because you're with me," Zeb explained, examining the hand-tooled belts hanging from a rack. "The last tourist who came to town was tarred and feathered." He raised two fingers in the air. "Scout's honor."

"I didn't know you were a Boy Scout," Chloe said as she plopped down in the wide woven hammock stretched between two poles in the middle of the store.

He walked over and gave the hammock a push. Chloe closed her eyes as she swung back and forth. He stared down at her, mesmerized by her copper-colored curls against the dark green fabric, noting her fair skin, dark lashes, freckled nose. Wondering how far the freckles extended, trying to remember.

"Sure am," he said absently. "Kind, courteous, brave, thrifty." He left out trustworthy. Didn't mention honest. On purpose. Good God, she was beautiful, lying there in that hammock that was big enough for two. What if he lay down next to her... What if the hammock formed a V, the way hammocks do, the contours of the fabric shoving them into each other's arms, the way hammocks do? Their hips would be thrust together, her breasts pushed against his chest. Their lips would meet, they'd exchange long, hot kisses, the kind he'd sampled that morning.

He'd rip her clothes off, she'd tear at his. Then, swinging back and forth in the middle of the dry-goods store, they'd make mad, passionate love all day long as customers came and went. He wiped a bead of perspiration off his forehead with his hand-kerchief.

He took a deep breath, reached out and grabbed the edge of the hammock and brought it to an abrupt halt. Her eyes flew open. "I almost fell asleep," she said, sighing so seductively his heart rate doubled.

If Wilma hadn't come back with an inflatable mat-tress in her arms he might have jumped right into that hammock and damn the consequences. That's how far gone he was. Gone crazy over some woman he didn't know and didn't want to know. He had to get away from her. Or better yet, she had to get away from him. Far, far away.

Chloe got up out of the hammock as if nothing had happened, bought the mattress and the hammock and, with his help, loaded everything into the back of his truck.

"I don't suppose…do they have a coffee shop around here or anything?" she asked.

"No," he said brusquely. "Just a bar."

"You don't think they have coffee in the bar, do you?" she asked wistfully.

"Absolutely not." He opened the passenger door to the truck and waited impatiently for her to get in.

"Why don't I just have a look," she said with a

certain stubborn look in her brown eyes he was beginning to recognize. And while he watched, she sashayed down the street and disappeared behind the swinging doors of the vintage Western bar, as if he didn't exist. As if he hadn't just told her they didn't serve coffee.

Now she'd find out they did. In fact, she was probably already sitting at the bar, surrounded by randy cowpunchers, ordering a double latte, or whatever the hell they drank in San Francisco. And drinking in the damaging information about Paradise Springs along with it.

He jammed his hat on his head and followed her down the street and through the swinging doors. He paused to let his eyes become accustomed to the gloom. She *was* sitting at the bar, sipping coffee from a thick ironstone mug with a blissful expression on her face. But she was alone except for Barney, who was polishing glasses behind the bar.

"Zeb," Barney said, putting the glass down. "Didn't expect you till Friday." He gestured to a poster advertising the weekend special: Live Music and Steak Dinners. Zeb flinched. He wanted to fling himself at the wall and block the picture of the sizzling steak platters and the band. But it was too late. She'd seen it.

"Imagine all this going on in a little town like this. I had no idea," she said, shooting an accusing glance in Zeb's direction, doubtless angry he hadn't let her in on the local excitement. "Why that sounds like fun," she said.

"Yep," Barney said. "Zeb had the idea about the

dinners. He's providing the meat. If it works, we'll do it every weekend. If it don't…"

Zeb knew what he was going to say. *"If it don't, we'll cancel the order for a hundred pounds of steak and let the musicians go."* But if it worked, it would provide Zeb and Sam a local outlet for their prize beef. It had to work. He was going to see to it that it worked, if he had to cook those steaks himself.

Chloe set her cup down and walked up so close to the poster he figured she must be nearsighted. "What time does the music start?" she asked.

"Late," Zeb said

"Can anyone come?" she asked over her shoulder.

"No. Invitation only," Zeb said, noting Barney's perplexed expression out of the corner of his eye.

Her big brown eyes widened, making her look so sad, so hurt, an ordinary man would have melted, invited her, offered her a ride. "Friday? You'll be…" He almost said "gone by then," but what if she wasn't? "You'll be too tired," he said instead.

She leaned against the wall, one hand on her hip, the other holding her cup. For one moment in the subdued light it looked like she was part of the poster, part of the band, part of the party. In reality, she was not part of anything. Except a big-city hospital.

"I sometimes stay up past nine," she told him. "After all, I'm a big girl." Her voice was as soft as a caress.

"I noticed," he muttered, his heart thudding against his ribs. He noticed everything about her. Noticed the way her jeans hugged her long, shapely legs. The way she licked her lips, leaving them wet and soft and kissable. She was a big girl and he was a big boy and he didn't like where this was heading.

He could see it now. He'd be flinging steaks on the grill in the kitchen while every single man in town was eyeing her, waiting for the opportunity to put the moves on her. And tell her all about the plans for her property. And nobody would be appreciating his prime aged beef. Damn her.

Why couldn't Horatio's only living relative have been an eighty-year-old widow with no desire to travel to the wilds of Colorado, instead of a shapely, heart-stopping wench with melting hot-chocolate eyes? Eyes that studied him over her coffee cup. Dark eyes that were brimming with understanding. That told him more than any words could that she understood there was some reason he didn't want her there on Friday, but that she was going to be there anyway.

"Aged prime beef courtesy of the Bowie Brothers." She read aloud from the poster.

He ignored the comment. "Ready?" with a pointed look at the cup in her hands.

Instead of setting her cup down and heading for the door, she took another sip and walked toward the bar. "What kind of music does the band play?" she asked, her back against the polished mahogany.

"Does it matter?" he growled. "Let's go."

But Barney had to put his two cents in. "Country, Western, whatever your pleasure."

Zeb glared at him. He'd like to leap over the bar, grab the towel out of Barney's hands and stuff it in his mouth. The guy hardly every said more than two words to a stranger. Now he wouldn't shut up.

"Great band," Barney said enthusiastically. "You gotta hear these guys, Miss...."

"Hudson. Chloe Hudson."

Barney reached across the bar and extended his hand. "Not any relation to Horatio?"

Zeb clenched his teeth. If he acted fast, he could still throw her over his shoulder, run down the street and dump her in the back of his truck.

But before he could move, she was shaking Barney's hand and saying, "I'm his great-grand-daughter."

"No kidding," Barney said.

"No kidding," Zeb echoed. "Now, if you're finished...I gotta be getting back."

"Of course." She turned to Barney. "Thanks for the coffee. I'll see you Friday. I'm looking forward to it."

Zeb breathed a sigh of relief. It could have been worse. Much worse. If he hadn't been there... if they'd continued their conversation...Barney might have spilled everything. He and Chloe walked down the boardwalk to the truck in silence. Zeb stared morosely into the distance, wondering how in the hell he was going to get rid of her, now that she had a sleeping bag and a hammock.

Chloe, on the other hand, had a spring to her step that belied her sleepless night. She'd discovered a bar straight out of the Old West, a bar with authentic music and hopefully real, authentic cowboys that would be an attraction for her guests, give them something to look forward to on the weekends. She'd check it out and write it up for her brochures.

So Zeb Bowie raised prime beef, and was entrepreneurial enough to sell it in town, getting his name out. Not just a tough rancher, she thought. Not just a gorgeous macho man who exuded sex appeal. He was a businessman too. But why didn't he want her to be there on Friday night, to hear the music and eat his steak? Was he afraid she'd get in his way? Come between him and someone else? After all, a guy like that was bound to have a girlfriend or two. She had to assure him she'd leave him alone. That she had no interest in him other than as a neighbor.

She glanced in his direction and was shocked by the rush of sexual desire that made her shiver in the warm summer air. She wanted to touch him. Badly. To plant her hands on his chest and feel his heartbeat through his shirt. Shove his hat off his head and tangle her hands in his sun-streaked hair again. But he had a girlfriend. He must have. That's why he didn't want her hanging around him on Friday night, looking at him like he was her dream of a cowboy come true. He was her neighbor. Nothing more, nothing less. She understood that. She really did.

"The bartender was friendly," she said, seeking a safe subject.

"He's not the bartender, he's the owner."

"Well, he couldn't have been nicer," she said.

"So you don't believe he was about to tar and feather you when I walked in and saved you."

She shook her head. "He didn't even think I was a tourist. Which I'm not."

He looked down at her. "Hah. New jeans. Ordering coffee instead of whiskey. You give yourself away every time you open your mouth. 'Can anyone come?''' he mimicked.

She flushed. "I don't care what you say. The people are nice."

He unlocked the door of the truck for her.

"I hate to take up any more of your time," she said, climbing into the passenger seat and wedging herself next to the door. "But I really need to pick up some food. Is there a grocery store anywhere around?"

"Nope," he said curtly. "Most people grow their own vegetables. Raise their own meat."

"What about a roadside stand? Or a farmers' market?"

"Saturday mornings."

"Oh."

"I guess we could swing by the co-op," he said reluctantly.

"It will only take a few minutes."

Chloe told him he didn't have to come into the store with her. She would have liked a few minutes to herself.

But he wouldn't leave her alone. He followed her around like a shadow while she forced herself to think about staples like rice and flour and powdered milk.

"You got enough stuff," he said once they were back in the truck.

"I realize I came woefully unprepared."

"For what?"

"To do what I want to do."

"You haven't told me what that is."

"You're sure you won't laugh? Scout's honor?" she asked.

He held up two fingers.

She took a deep breath. "I want to make the resort into a health spa."

"Paradise Springs a fat farm?" He threw his head back and roared with laughter. "A fat farm, that's good. You're not serious?"

Chloe took a deep breath. She clenched her hands into fists, and turned to glare at him. "You promised," she said. "How could you? You're no Boy Scout, are you?"

"I'm sorry," he said, trying to stifle a grin. "I couldn't help it. I thought those quote, *spas*, unquote, were luxurious resorts where women went to get pampered and maybe lose a few pounds."

"They are. And there's no reason why Paradise Hot Springs can't be one of those."

"There isn't? What about the long hike in, the lack of kitchen facilities, bathrooms or bedrooms?"

"Those are problems," she admitted, "but they are solvable."

"With a whole lot of money. Do you have a whole lot of money?"

"That's none of your business."

He shrugged. "Just trying to be helpful."

"I don't think you are. I think you're trying to discourage me so I'll sell you the property."

"I'm trying to get you to be realistic." He turned onto the dirt road past the hand-carved Bar Z Ranch sign.

"Thank you," she said stiffly. "But I've been re-alistic all my life. I chose nursing because it was a safe profession. Nurses can always get jobs. I married a doctor thinking I'd have a secure future. And now because of great-grandpa, I have a chance to do something new and different and exciting, and nobody's going to stop me from fulfilling my dream. Not you, not anybody.'' She bit her lip and her eyes filled with tears.

Zeb froze. She was married. To a doctor. Doctors made a lot of money. More than ranchers, anyway. So that's what she meant when she'd said "I'm not independently wealthy, although..."

He felt like a fool for kissing her, for fantasizing about making love to her. Why hadn't she told him, why wasn't she wearing a ring, and why did she kiss him back? Because she was a thrill-seeker, looking for something new and different and exciting.

He maneuvered the truck around potholes, gripping the steering wheel so tightly his knuckles turned white as the truth finally hit home. She was going to turn Paradise Hot Springs into a damned spa for fat women. She was not going to sell him the property. She had deep pockets. And she was married, for God's sake.

"Here we are," he said, slamming on the brakes at the fork in the road.

She hesitated for just a moment and shot him a brief, puzzled glance before letting herself out. "I'll unload my stuff here and then carry it down to my place," she decided.

"You do that," he said, killing the motor and staying in his seat behind the wheel. Why should he help her unload her things? Where was her husband? In the operating room? So she had a dream. Well, he had a dream, too. To buy Paradise Springs for a reasonable figure. To resell it for a profit and buy a bull who would put him back in business. A dream of holding on to his ranch. A dream that was fading into nothingness.

He watched her in the rearview mirror as she struggled with the boxes and bags until he couldn't stand it any more. Then he got out of the truck, slammed his door shut and, in tension-filled silence, grabbed box after box out of the rear and dropped them unceremoniously onto the ground next to the trail that led to Paradise Springs. When he finished, there was a pile of stuff so high it would take her about three months to haul to her property.

"Thank you," she said, wiping the perspiration off her forehead. She looked tired, but undaunted. He should have known the first moment he saw her yesterday, that she was the type who didn't give up. He should have known she was married, too. A woman who could sleep on the ground, ride a horse for the first time and still look like a million dollars *would* be married. As usual, he was a day late and a dollar short. No, a few years late and about fifty-thousand dollars short was more like it.

Chloe stood there, breathing hard, her breasts rising and falling beneath her cotton shirt. "I don't understand you," she said at last.

She didn't understand *him?* Frustration built and threatened to swamp him. "Would this help?" he asked, grabbing her by one arm and hauling her up against him. His fingers tightened around her wrist in a bruising grip. Ignoring her effort to pull away, he jerked her into his arms. He didn't imagine the thudding of her heart against his. It was real. He didn't mistake the look in her eyes for curiosity. He recognized desire, hot, pure and simple. It matched his own.

His hands moved to her hips, cupping her buttocks, pulling her against his aching erection. She wrapped her arms around him. He kissed her, and with matching fervor she kissed him back. Over and over, as if she wanted him as much as he wanted her. As if she was just as aroused and frustrated as he was.

Her sighs, her soft moans made his blood boil. Her tongue tangled with his. He could take her down on the ground with him right now, make love under the trees, everything else forgotten—her refusal to sell him the land, and the fact that she wasn't free. This was madness. She was *married*. But she sure as hell didn't act as if she was.

Abruptly he dropped his arms and backed away. "You don't understand *me?*" he demanded.

"That's right," she said as she stumbled backwards, rubbing her mouth with the back of her hand as if to erase his kisses. "And that didn't help at all."

Four

Adrenaline pumped through her body as Chloe carried the first box down the trail and through the woods to the old resort. It might have weighed twenty pounds, it might have weighed fifty. She was oblivious. She was so mad at Zebulon Bowie she could spit. How had she let this happen?

And all she knew was that she was not going to accept one more favor from the randy, dominating, insulting cowboy she had the misfortune to live next door to. Not if she starved and they found her bones at the end of the summer. Not if she sprained her ankle and lay helpless on the bare ground. She wouldn't call him for help. And if he stumbled on her by accident, she'd close her eyes and play dead before she'd let him help her to her feet.

Not that she was going to starve or sprain her ankle, she told herself as she planted one foot after the other on the rough ground. She could take care of herself. She had supplies. She was in good health. She had confidence. Yes, she did. She didn't need him to provide her with food, or rides. She didn't need help carrying her supplies in from the road. She was glad he hadn't offered, because then she would have had to refuse.

She just wished she'd taken a moment to decide which box to carry in first. But she couldn't. Not and retain her dignity. Because he was watching her. Waiting for her to stumble. To fail. Then he'd close in on her like a mountain lion after a deer and snatch away her property.

If she had taken a moment, she would have chosen the box with the hammock or the groceries. Because by the time she got back to the bathhouse next to the stream, it was dusk and her arms ached. It was no problem to hike back to where her boxes sat, no problem at all. On the other hand, it would feel so good to stretch out in that tub and let the steaming waters work their magic on her aching muscles, then heat something over her new propane camp stove and rock herself to sleep in her new hammock.

She dumped the box on the ground and rubbed the muscles in her arms. Then she tore at the cardboard with her fingernails. It was her hammock and the stove. Thank heavens. Even if she didn't get back to pick up the rest of the stuff tonight, she'd at least have a hot meal and a good night's sleep. And after a hot meal and a good night's sleep, she could do anything. Without anyone's help, she thought smugly.

From the supply of freeze-dried food in her suitcase, she chose turkey tetrazzini, added springwater, lit the stove and sat cross-legged on the ground in front of it. When it was hot she ate every reconstituted noodle and every shred of turkey, then washed it down with cold mountain springwater. Her very own water, from her very own spring. She sighed with contentment, satisfied with her self-sufficiency.

She wished Zeb Bowie could see her now. He'd see how well she fit into the Rocky Mountain lifestyle. So she'd ordered the wrong drink at the bar and maybe she had said the wrong thing to the bartender. That didn't mean she didn't belong there. She belonged there as much as anyone. Maybe more than anyone. Because her great-grandfather was a pioneer, and she'd inherited his spirit.

Filled with turkey tetrazzini and a new confidence, she unwrapped her new hammock and tied it between two trees. It was made of strong canvas and she was very tired. After pulling on an extra sweatshirt, she rolled into the hammock. Her stomach, full of springwater and freeze-dried turkey, lurched as she swung between the trees. If she hadn't known she was landlocked, she would have sworn she was seasick. She threw one leg over the edge of the hammock and dug her toe into the ground to stop its movement. Then, ever so carefully, she lifted her leg and tucked it back. The breeze picked up and she was swinging back and forth again. She moaned and buried her face in the stiff canvas and closed her eyes.

The wind blew out of the west and tossed her from side to side. Tiny rain drops began to fall gently on the back of her head and her shoulders. Soon her whole body was wet. She rolled out of the hammock.

"All right, I give up," she muttered and shuffled back to the bathhouse for the second straight night. Only this time she didn't gaze up at the stars through the slats above her head, she stared at the rain that splatted intermittently against her forehead like a Chinese torture. Finally, somehow, she drifted off into a damp, uncomfortable sleep.

Zeb was uncomfortable, too. Not that he was damp. He was warm and dry on the second floor of the old house as he listened to the rain on the shake roof. But he couldn't help thinking of those cardboard boxes stacked on the side of the road—and the woman who'd left them there. The woman who'd stomped away without a backward glance, with a huge box in her arms, a box she could barely see over. He wondered how she made it back without stumbling in those flimsy sandals. Even if she had, the rest of the boxes and bags must still be there. There was no way she could have carried them all the way back to the springs. So right now the cardboard was probably disintegrating into pulp, leaving her new survival equipment exposed to the elements.

Not to mention her groceries, which were turning to mush. The twenty-five-pound bag of flour would be paste by now. The sugar would be dissolving into syrup and running off like snow melt. He should be happy about that. Without food she couldn't survive. She'd have to leave. The very thought should have made him smile. But it didn't.

He stood at the window in his boxer shorts and stared out at the rain. He *wanted* her to leave.

There was no doubt in his mind that she was destined to fail. Eventually. Because he knew something about failure. And he knew that it was okay to fail if you'd done your damnedest to succeed. She hadn't had a chance to do that yet.

There was nothing he wanted more than to see her walking back down the trail from where she came, in her silk shirt and suede boots. But not without a go at it. Not without trying. Why not give her a fighting chance? Would it be that hard to haul her stuff down to the springs and store them in a cabin? The answer was yes, but he did it anyway. He led two of his pack mules down to the road in the rain, loaded all of her goods onto their backs and into their saddlebags and led the way by horseback down the trail, with the rain beating a tattoo on the hood of his parka. And the voice in his head said, "You're a fool, Bowie. A stupid idiot. You think she'll thank you for this and then leave? Is that the deal? Think again."

It was coming down hard now. The trail was pure mud and the mules brayed their protest. He felt like braying himself. But he kept going. When they finally reached the springs, he tossed her boxes on the dirt floor of a deserted cabin. He had no idea what condition her groceries were in. That was for her to find out. He'd done enough for her already. Too much.

He looked around at the old pool, slowly filling with rain water. Noticed the hammock swinging in the wind. Stood there wondering where she was. In

one of the other cabins? In the bathhouse? Back in
San Francisco? No, that would be too good to be
true. Wherever she was, he didn't plan to see her
again. He would send her a message. How he would
do that, he didn't know. There was no mail delivery
at the springs. And carrier pigeon was out.

Sam. He'd wait a day or two and he'd have Sam
make her their final offer. By then, she'd be ready to
accept. By then, Sam would see what a misfit she
was. What a gorgeous, gutsy, misfit she was. Which
was why he was not going to see her again. There
was something about her that made it hard for him
to stick to his principles. Something about the way
she looked at him, with a mixture of stubborn pride
and vulnerability. Which was why this was the last,
the positively last thing he was going to do with her
or for her.

What if Sam didn't see what a misfit she was? He
had this tendency to feel sorry for poor, defenseless
creatures. Poor, defenseless Chloe Hudson? Hah!
He'd have to think of something else. He didn't even
want Sam to meet her.

He thought so long and so far into the night that
he overslept the next morning. Small wonder, since
he'd been out in the rain half the night and spent the
other half worrying. At least he'd had no dreams
about Chloe Hudson to interfere with his rest. She
was out of his dreams. Now if only he could get her
out of his mind and out of his life. He might still
have been sleeping if George, his foreman hadn't
pounded on his bedroom door.

"Boss, you in there? Somebody here to see you."

"What? What time is it? Who is it?" Zeb staggered across the room and opened the door.

"It's a lady," George said in a stage whisper, his eyes wide with shock.

Zeb rocked back on his bare heels. "No further questions. Tell her I'm not here," he whispered urgently. "Tell her I left the country."

"But...I already asked her in for a cup of coffee and a biscuit. She looked so puny, like she could use a bite. She's sittin' at the kitchen table right now," George added with a nervous glance over his shoulder.

Zeb closed his eyes for a moment, hoping he was dreaming this part. But when he opened them, George was still standing there, staring at him. "Okay, okay, I'm coming," he assured him.

Zeb dragged his feet as he came down the stairs and approached the kitchen. It wasn't too late to sneak out the front door. On the other hand, maybe she'd come to say goodbye. He didn't want to miss that. Besides, he was hungry. And George's biscuits were worth waking up for.

Evidently she thought so too, because she was sitting at the table with a thick mug of steaming coffee in front of her, watching George take a pan out of the oven. The kitchen was warm and steamy, fragrant with the smell of his hot, flaky biscuits.

But the minute Chloe looked up at him, and her gaze collided with his, he forgot about food and remembered the way she'd kissed him at the edge of the road. The way she sighed and moaned with reckless abandon, letting him think...letting him imagine what might come next. He squeezed his eyes shut and forcibly blocked the image. But he couldn't forget the way she'd wrapped her arms around him and opened her lips to welcome him in as if there was no tomorrow.

But there *was* tomorrow. Tomorrow was now. He had to get rid of her. Now.

"Here you are, little lady," George said, sliding a half dozen biscuits onto a plate in front of her.

Zeb shot daggers at his old friend and foreman but George seemed oblivious. "Wait a minute," Zeb said. "She can't eat all those. What about me?"

"Plenty more where those came from," George said with a grin that showed his gold front tooth. Then with a deliberate wink in the direction of his employer, he left the room.

The room was silent, except for the coffee percolating on the stove. Zeb reached for a cup. What in the hell was she doing there? It was bad enough she'd taken over his hot tub, now she'd invaded his kitchen as well. He snuck a glance at her out of the corner of his eye. And noted with satisfaction that she looked tired. Why he should feel a stab of sympathy in the vicinity of his gut, was beyond comprehension. Maybe it was just hunger. Yeah, that's what it was.

The next time he looked at her there was a faint blush on her cheeks. She looked embarrassed. She should be embarrassed.

"I didn't come here for breakfast," she explained.

"You could have fooled me," Zeb grumbled, pouring himself a cup of coffee since it looked like no one was going to do it for him.

"I came to thank you," she said, "and—"

"Forget it." He sat across from her, took a biscuit off her plate and slathered it with butter and honey.

Chloe studied him from under long lashes. She only wished she could look that good first thing in the morning. Maybe after she had her inflatable mattress set up she would. For now she felt like her back was in a vise. Her eyelids were heavy and red around the rims.

Not him. His eyes were the clear blue of the ocean outside the Golden Gate, though he must have spent hours in the night bringing her goods down the trail to the springs. He moved around the kitchen with the grace of a panther. And he ate like a bear, putting away biscuits one after the other. Everyone she knew at home watched what they ate. A plain bagel for breakfast, a salad for lunch and lean meat for dinner. This man did hard physical work all day. It showed in every muscle of his physique. He was quite a specimen. She'd noticed that right away as he stood there in the bathhouse, in all his naked glory. She stared into her coffee cup as if there might be a message in the grounds. If there was, it would surely say: *Don't get carried away. You're in a vulnerable state. Just divorced, away from friends and family. Tired, hungry and depressed.*

But there was no denying he was a beautiful man. On the outside. If you liked the rugged type, that is. It was the inside she didn't understand. What made him tick? Why had he driven away in a huff, leaving her with a stack of boxes, only to return in the middle of the night to haul them to the resort?

"As I said before," she murmured, "I don't understand you."

"What's not to understand?" he said, lifting his cup in the air. "I didn't want to see your stuff dissolve in the rain. Call it thrift. Call it prudence."

"I call it kindness."

He glared at her. "Well, don't."

She hesitated, afraid to offend him again with another compliment. "Look," she said, "I know you don't want me here. I shouldn't have come and barged in on your breakfast like this. But I don't have a phone, and I was grateful and the biscuits smelled so good."

"All the way over to the springs?"

"No...no. I mean when I got to the door. But now that I know you don't want to be thanked, I just..."

"You got that right."

"I just want to say, I was hoping maybe we could get along somehow. As neighbors, maybe friends and..."

"What about the doctor?"

"Doctor? Are you sick?"

"I'm not sick. But I'm not stupid, either. And I don't like being used. As some kind of substitute."

Her face wrinkled into a puzzled frown. "What?"

"You're married."

She set her mug down with a thud. "No, I'm not. I was, but I'm not anymore." She tried for a casual, I-don't-care tone and it almost worked. If her lip hadn't quivered it would have. The truth was that she did care. She cared that her marriage had failed. She cared that she'd put so much into it and had nothing to show for it. Nothing but a determination not to let it happen again. She pressed her lips together. No more quivering. No more tears.

"What happened?" he asked, bracing his elbows on the old pine table.

She almost told him it was none of his business. But there was something in his eyes. It wasn't sympathy. She hated sympathy. That was why she'd left San Francisco. Everybody felt so sorry for her. Even if they didn't say anything. It was there in their eyes.

It wasn't understanding, either. How could he possibly understand? He didn't know her. He didn't know Brandon. It was just interest. Interest in her, as a neighbor, and in her story. Was that what she was looking for? Was that what she'd come a thousand miles to find?

She took a sip of coffee, then gazed off over his head and out the window to the barn and the fields beyond. She never intended to tell a stranger the story of her marriage, but somehow the words tumbled out. "He wanted some space," she said.

"Space?"

"Yes, you know. He felt like he'd been crowded all his life. His parents pushed him to succeed, first to get into the right college, then medical school, internship, residency. It was nonstop work, work, work, for years and years."

"Tell me about it," Zeb muttered.

"And now that he's made it, he's got his own practice, and money coming in, he wants to live a little."

"And you don't?" he asked.

"Of course, but in a different way. He, uh, he wants to go out with other women. He *is* going out with other women. *Was* going out with other women." Once those words spoken aloud would have filled her with humiliation. Now, just getting them out into the air gave her a feeling of relief.

"Not exactly conducive to a good marriage," Zeb said dryly.

"No. Are you...speaking from experience?" she asked hesitantly. She expected him to tell her it was none of her business. But she hated spilling her guts to someone she knew so little about.

"No. But I came close once. And I've observed some happy marriages and some unhappy ones. It doesn't take a rocket scientist to know you can't cheat. There goes love. There goes trust. Out the window." He glanced out the open window over the kitchen sink at the gray skies. Then he stood abruptly and closed it with a loud bang, as if that would keep love and trust inside. It signaled an end to the conversation. "And now if you'll excuse me."

"Of course. I'm keeping you from your work. I just wanted..."

"To thank me, I know." He took his hat from the rack and reached for the door.

"Not only that," she said running her damp palms down the sides of her jeans. What was wrong with her, a seasoned San Francisco hostess, accustomed to giving dinner parties for twelve, afraid to ask one cowboy to dinner? If she didn't speak now, he'd be out the door in a second. "I was wondering if you'd like to come to dinner tonight." There, she'd said it.

"Dinner?" he asked, stupefied.

"Yes, dinner. Now that I've got my supplies, I wanted to celebrate. And I owe you for the other night and now for breakfast. It won't be elaborate, all I've got is the little stove, but I thought I

could…'' She was blathering. Unable to stop. Afraid
if she did, he'd say no. For some reason it was ter-
ribly important for him to say yes. If she kept talking,
he'd keep standing there with his hand on the doorknob, staring at her as if she was asking him to go
hang gliding from Sheep Mountain. ''Of course, if
you're busy…''

''I am pretty busy,'' he said and pushed the door
open halfway.

Her heart sank. The tears she'd been holding back
sprang to her eyes. Why, because a neighbor was too
busy to come to dinner? Come on. She forced her
lips to form a quavery smile and walked to the door,
where she turned sideways and brushed by him on
her way out. And in that split second, the tips of her
breasts came into contact with the hard muscles in
his chest.

She froze. She wanted to move. To get away from
him and his kitchen and his ranch. But she couldn't.
Their faces were so close she could see the faint
worry lines in his forehead. See the rough shadow of
a beard that lined his jaw. Almost feel how it would
scrape across her face.

''Sorry,'' she said under her breath. Surprised that
she could speak at all. Surprised she could breathe.

Zeb grabbed her by the shoulders, intending to
push her away. Instead he groaned and pulled her
tight against him. So tight he could feel her full
breasts pressed against his chest. Her hips locked
onto his. So close she must be aware of his hot, un-
mistakable arousal. What must she think of him?
Turning her out of his house, then holding on to her
so she couldn't leave? He didn't know. He didn't

care. He wanted her. He wanted her to go. He wanted her to stay. God help him, he just wanted her.

He lowered his lips until they were just a whisper away from hers. He looked into her eyes, searching for something. Red light or green. What he saw was red-hot desire that matched his own. He reminded himself that this woman was standing between him and everything he wanted. But at that moment he didn't want anything as much as he wanted her. The air was thick with tension. Then he couldn't take it any longer.

He kissed her. She kissed him back. She leaned forward and he leaned back until his spine was pressed against the side of the house. Her lips were sticky and tasted like honey. Maybe his did, too. If so, they might be stuck together forever. He trailed his callused fingers down her back then cupped her firm bottom in his broad hands to bring her even closer.

She made a little purring sound of pleasure, then paused to lick the honey off her lips. Then off his lips. Causing a rapid increase in his heart rate until his libido couldn't take it any more. Until all he could think about was his warm bed upstairs and how much he wanted to carry her up there and smear honey all over his body just to see if she could lick it all off.

"Boss. Boss, you still here?" George yelled from the general direction of the barn.

He opened his mouth to answer but no sound came out, only the hoarse breathing of an aroused male. Until Chloe broke out of his arms. Then he tried again. "Yeah," he said.

"There's somebody to see you. Something about a bull."

Good. Something about a bull. Nobody comes to the ranch for a week, it's usually just him and George and some part-time help. But today it's a regular Grand Central Station. Thank God, because he didn't want to be alone with Chloe. Not at all. Before he went to see who it was, Chloe turned on her heel, and without a word, walked down the path toward the hot springs. He had no idea if she was mad, sad or as turned on as he was. He thought she'd say something—like "See ya," or "Don't forget about tonight."

What was he supposed to do about dinner? Nothing. That's what he was supposed to do. Pretend she hadn't asked him. Pretend she hadn't kissed him. Forget she melted in his arms like butter on a hot biscuit. Forget about the rush of relief he felt when she told him she wasn't married. Forget about her entirely. Yeah, right.

Chloe had plenty to do. In addition to the sleeping bag, the mattress, the hammock, the stove and the groceries, she'd bought cleaning supplies. As she scrubbed the inside of the nicest cabin, if you could call any of them nice, she had a little talk with herself.

She reminded herself that she was very susceptible. That she'd recently been rejected and that it was only natural that she should want to prove she was still attractive to men. But this wasn't the way to do it. Not with a cowboy who was amusing himself by flirting with the new girl in town. No matter how sexy and desirable he made her feel, she was not his type and he was not hers.

But, oh, the way he made her feel. Could anything that felt that good be all bad? Yes! She picked up her wire brush and scrubbed the old planked floor of the cabin so hard she took off a layer of old paint with the dirt. Her goal was to turn this resort into a spa. That a sexy cowboy thought it was a ridiculous idea only made her more determined to make it succeed. She would never again sacrifice her own goals for someone else's. She'd worked hard to put Brandon through those last years of school. Thanks to her and to his parents, he had no debts to pay off. Thanks to his dumping her, she would never trust or love again. On the other hand, thanks to his dumping her, she was here in Colorado embarking on a new adventure.

She didn't know if Zeb was coming to dinner or not. It didn't matter one way or the other. She was cooking anyway—outside, if it didn't rain. And if it did...there was her cabin. Her newly scrubbed, empty cabin. There was no furniture in it, but all she needed was her mattress, the supplies she'd bought and her suitcase. If it rained, she'd sit on the mattress and eat off her lap.

If her friends could see her now. Planning a dinner next to a mountain stream, sitting on a rock eating off a tin plate. She who'd once given elegant dinner parties in a town house overlooking the Bay Bridge, and worried about who would sit next to whom. That wouldn't be a problem tonight. Even if he came. But he wouldn't. Hadn't she gotten the message? He was busy.

She didn't care, she told herself as she soaked in her extra-long tub in her very own bathhouse. She changed her clothes, from old dirty jeans and a T-shirt to a fresh T-shirt and a clean pair of jeans. Not for him. For herself. Then she made a fire the way she'd seen him do it, and lit her camp stove as well. That way she could have a two-pot dinner. For one.

She was so intent on opening boxes, measuring powdered milk and stirring the sauce, she didn't hear him approach. When she finally looked up from the fire, he was standing there. Her gaze traveled slowly over him, starting with his scuffed boots, to his clean, well-worn jeans and on to his freshly shaved, rugged face and clean hair that brushed the collar of his blue denim shirt. She dropped her measuring cup and promptly forgot what she was doing. She wished he'd given her some warning, like snapping a few twigs underfoot, or discreetly coughing, so she could have steeled herself for his arrival. There ought to be a law against anyone sneaking through the forest and looking that good, in the morning, in the evening, in town and in the country.

"Looks good," he said.

She dumped the ingredients together, gave them a stir, and got to her feet. Then wished she hadn't. Her knees buckled. He reached out to steady her, then dropped his arms as quickly as if he'd been scalded.

"You didn't say what time," he said.

"You didn't say you were coming."

"I wasn't sure I'd be able to." He held out a bottle of wine.

"Thank you. How nice."

"Not sure how nice. Found it in the cellar. Might have been there a good while," he said.

"Have you lived here long?"

"All my life. The land has been in the family for three generations. The wine may have been, too. Let's open it and see." He pulled a corkscrew from his back pocket and removed the cork, then he poured generous portions into two tin cups and handed her one.

"Here's to Paradise Springs," he said.

"And to Grandpa Hudson."

"May he rest in peace," he said respectfully.

Chloe sipped slowly, letting the flavor wrap around her tongue. He did the same.

"Spicy," she said, looking at him over her cup.

"Earthy," he returned, his brazen gaze lingering on the swell of her breasts.

"Plummy with tangy acidity," she retorted, feeling her skin tingle as the wine slid down her throat.

"And a long, smooth finish," he added with a gleam in his eye.

She swallowed hard and caught her breath. She was warm. So very warm. Heat suffused her body. And it wasn't from the fire or the little stove. This was an inner heat she couldn't' damp down or turn off. She could only move away from the source. She stepped back and folded her arms over her chest as if she was shielding herself from the sensual heat emanating from this sexy, flirtatious cowboy.

"How do you know so much…about wine?"

"I've been around a little. But I'd like to do some more tasting. How about you? Care to join me?"

His voice was as smooth and seductive as the

wine. They both knew what kind of tasting he was suggesting. She reminded herself to be careful. He was not quite the country bumpkin she'd first thought. And she was not as in control of the situation as she'd like to be. Wisely, she left his question unanswered.

"I thought we'd start with salad," she said, bending down to heap some lettuce with an oil-and-vinegar dressing onto a metal plate for him.

He looked at it suspiciously for a moment, as if he was about to make some remark about rabbit food, but after she'd served herself and joined him on a log at the fireside, he dug in and cleaned his plate in minutes.

"Where'd you learn to cook?" he asked, leaning lazily back on his elbows to watch her stir the piquant mixture on the stove.

"Just trial and error. When I got married I couldn't boil an egg. Before I left I could throw together dinner for twelve."

Zeb accepted a plate full of pasta with a rich, creamy sauce on it and shook his head in amazement. Not at the fact that she could cook dinner for twelve, but that her husband, the doctor, could let her go. Somebody who looked like that and cooked like that? He didn't get it.

"What was it, some kind of midlife crisis he had?" he asked.

"I guess you could call it that." She paused. "You said you came close to getting married."

"Did I?" he asked. Why had he said that? He didn't want to talk about it. He didn't want to think about it.

"This morning. You talked about love and trust."

He shook his head. "Not me. I never talk about love and trust."

"Well, you did," she said, refilling his cup.

He took a long drink then set his cup down. "It's a long story."

She leaned back against a fir tree. "I'm not going anywhere."

Five

It might have been the wine. It might have been the food. It might have been her, looking at him across the fire with her big brown eyes, the flickering light turning her hair to gold and her skin to bronze. Sitting there patiently waiting for him to talk. Whatever it was, he told her about Joanne, his high-school sweetheart. About how they'd been the perfect couple. Until she left town with the propane-delivery man.

"Just like that?" Chloe asked. "Without any warning?"

"Plenty of warning. Everyone warned me. But I was too blind to see. To deaf to hear what I should have known," he said soberly. "All those nights she was busy. Besides, she was a town girl. Never did feel quite comfortable out here. I thought after I got the place fixed up, she'd like it better. But she didn't. She thought it was too quiet. Too far from town. Too far from friends.''

"But you've got a nice house. It feels lived in," Chloe said.

"It has been. By three generations of Bowies. I thought there'd be at least three more. Maybe there will be. That's up to my brother now." He set his plate on the ground and brushed his hands together.

"Why? There must be someone else for you. I understand you're quite popular."

"Popular, yes. Someone else, no. Not for me. I'd always wonder, I'd always be afraid she'd leave." He stared into the dying embers. "Nope. What do they say? Fool me once, shame on you. Fool me twice, shame on me. I won't take another chance." There was a long silence where the sadness and the self-pity threatened to come rushing back. But he shook off the cobwebs of memory and stretched his arms over his head. Regarding her with narrowed eyes, he said, "I don't know why I'm telling you all this."

"Sometimes it's easier to talk to a stranger," she said.

"Maybe. I know I haven't mentioned her name in two years. Thought I'd forgotten her." God knew he'd tried.

"I got the impression from the clerk in the general store that you were something of a ladies' man."

"Don't believe everything you hear."

"You mean you don't go out with women?"

"Of course I go out with women. I just don't get serious. And neither do they. Works out fine. Probably it was all for the best, Joanne's leaving. She knew something I didn't know at the time. I'm not the marrying kind."

"I guess that's how I feel, too," she said. "I've had enough marriage to last the rest of my life."

"I can't believe that," he said, stretching his legs out toward the fire and looking at her with amazement. "Somebody else will come along and snap you up. Because he was a fool to let you go."

Her eyes widened. "That must be the wine talking. That's the nicest thing you've said to me."

Uh-oh. What had he done? Gone and made a personal remark to his neighbor. It meant nothing, but she might think it did. Now it was time to go home. Now, before he got sentimental and said something else. He set his cup on the ground and stood, feeling just a tad unsteady on his feet. The wine might be talking, but the wine was going to have a hard time walking. He took a step backward and tripped over a root.

Alarmed, she reached out to take his arm. "Are you okay?" she asked. The concern in her voice was touching.

He took her arms and looked into her eyes. "I'm fine," he said. God, she was beautiful by firelight. She was beautiful, sympathetic and understanding, too. She even smelled good. Like flowers. Even though there wasn't a flower within spitting distance. Why did she have to inherit the land he wanted? If she was just some tourist they could have one hell of a fling this summer. Because he had a feeling it might be just what she needed. Him, too. A summer romance to end all summer romances. Something to remember. Or forget. Whatever.

"I could walk you home," she offered, drawing her delicate eyebrows together.

"But then I'd have to walk you back," he said.

"On account of all those bobcats and mountain lions?"

He nodded. "Or I could stay right here in your hammock. With you." He paused, watching her, waiting for her reaction. He loved to see her get mad. See her eyes flash and her face turn red. But she didn't get mad. Not this time. A series of emotions crossed her face. Maybe she was tempted to say yes. Or was that just wishful thinking? "That way nobody has to walk anybody anywhere," he said with an engaging smile, as if it was the most logical solution.

"I don't think so," she said with a determined lift of her chin. "I didn't come to Colorado to indulge in some romantic fantasy."

"I know. You came to make a fat farm out of a broken-down hot-springs resort. Thanks for reminding me. And thanks for the dinner." He reached for his hat, and slammed it tight onto his head. "Good night."

He stumbled more than once on his way home, strayed off the trail in the dark and bumped into more than one tree. What a night. He'd drunk too much wine. Her fault, for refilling his cup. He'd spilled his guts to a woman he didn't know. Her fault again. She'd acted so sympathetic, so understanding. *Easier to talk to a stranger,* she said. So easy he found himself talking about matters that were no concern of hers.

Then he'd made an overture and he'd been rejected. But hadn't she encouraged him by inviting him to dinner? Discussed the wine with him, with every remark having a double meaning? What did she expect after a dinner like that? Oh well, it was just as well. He could not get involved with the great-granddaughter of Horatio Hudson. He could just hear old Horatio now.

"Hands off my great-granddaughter, boy. I want her to have the place. Want her to do what I couldn't do. Restore Paradise Springs to its former glory."

"But Horatio," Zeb mumbled as he staggered toward his house, "She's a city girl. She can't even ride a horse. She's afraid of heights. She drinks coffee in a bar. She doesn't belong here. Horatio," he called desperately, glancing up at the sky. "Did you hear me? Give me a sign that you want *me* to have your land." The clouds raced across the sky and blocked the moon from view. But Horatio, wherever he was, was silent.

On top of everything, Zeb was no closer to his goal than he'd been two days ago. He could only pray Chloe Hudson would run out of steam before she found out what he knew. What everybody knew. Everybody but her. That the Bureau of Reclamation was planning to build a dam upstream from the hot springs and flood her property. That whoever owned the property could turn a tidy profit by selling to the Bureau.

The next morning when his head pounded in time to a distant drummer, thanks to that spicy, earthy wine he'd consumed the night before, Zeb decided to give Paradise Springs a wide berth for a few days. He was just a mite embarrassed about spilling the story of his broken engagement. Still didn't understand how it had happened. It had to be the wine. Of course it was the wine. But he'd had wine before and never been tempted to tell a total stranger how he'd been dumped. Maybe it was knowing she'd been hurt, too. Knowing they had something in common. It didn't matter. Hopefully she'd forgotten all about it by now.

He assumed Chloe had enough supplies so that she wouldn't be likely to go to town any time soon. Which meant there was no danger of her hearing any gossip. And who would be coming out to see her? Nobody.

If she didn't give up out of sheer loneliness, overwhelmed by the enormity of the job she faced, then he didn't understand city women. So all he had to do was to keep away from her and let her come to a decision on her own. The right decision. The only decision that made any sense. To sell the place and go back where she belonged.

It wouldn't be hard to stay away from Paradise Springs. Oh, he'd miss his nightly soak in the therapeutic waters that felt so good after a hard day in the saddle. But God knew he had enough work to do on his own place. After letting most of his crew go to save money, he had to do most of the branding, roping, breeding, calving on his own. He was especially busy now, with Sam on the road.

In the following days he occasionally thought about his neighbor, remembering, in spite of himself, how at home she'd looked at his breakfast table, scarfing down his biscuits. How delicious she'd tasted after breakfast. And how much he'd wanted to pursue her. Right up the stairs to his bedroom. How frustrated he felt every time he saw her. Frustrated that she wouldn't sell out to him. Frustrated that he hadn't gone to bed with her. Yet.

He wondered what she was up to. She was surely discouraged by now. Maybe she'd even gone home. Without saying goodbye? Why not? She didn't owe him a goodbye. She didn't owe him anything. Just the transfer of land would be sufficient. But that didn't require him to see her again. See her damp curls splayed against the edge of a white enamel tub. See her cheeks flush from the heat of the fire. Feel her snug bottom pressed against his masculinity.

No. All future communication could be, would be and should be done by mail.

By Friday Chloe was tired, but satisfied. She'd scrubbed, she hauled, she'd lifted and cleared and pulled. Maybe no one else would see the difference in the place, but she did. She was looking forward to going to town tonight. Hearing the music. Eating something she hadn't cooked on a camp stove—like a steak from the Bar Z Ranch. Meeting some new people. Seeing some she already knew.

All right, so she was looking forward to seeing Zeb. She'd missed him these past few days. He was amusing and entertaining. She never knew what he'd do or say next. But she couldn't expect him to come by every evening and entertain her. That's why she was looking forward to tonight. After a hot soak and a change of clothes, she hiked out by the same trail she'd come in by. Was it only five days ago? It seemed like eons. The trail was a little shorter, maybe because it was all downhill. She didn't want to think about climbing back up to the springs later that night. Even with her flashlight, it wouldn't be a picnic. Still, she had to go out. She had cabin fever.

She never had understood what Zeb meant about the people in Powderkeg. If anything, they were friendlier than ever. Wilma waved to her from the window of the dry-goods store.

"Looks like you could use a good pair of hiking boots," she said when Chloe stopped to say hello.

"That's right," Chloe said, feeling a new blister on her heel. "It's a long walk out of the property to my car."

"Thought you'd be hitching a ride from Zeb," Wilma said pulling some boxes down from a shelf.

"Me? Oh, no. I...I hardly know him. Haven't seen him for days...have you?" Now why did she have to ask that? As if she cared.

"Saw his truck go by just a few minutes ago. In the direction of the bar. Getting ready for tonight, I expect. You're staying for the food and the music, aren't you? Everybody who's anybody will be there. That includes you," Wilma said kindly, holding out a lightweight hiking boot for Chloe's inspection.

Chloe flushed with pleasure. After Zeb's warnings, she was doubly pleased to be included in the category of everybody-who's-anybody. Wilma made her feel almost like she belonged. She bought two pairs of boots, some new stonewashed jeans, T-shirts, a hat and a pair of khaki shorts. All the while, she pictured the new business she'd bring to Wilma when she got her spa going. She'd bring her guests here and they'd go wild with the leather belts, cotton scarves and checkered shirts. After she stashed her purchases in the trunk of her car, she ambled down Main Street, looking in windows at tractors, tools and other heavy equipment.

It was way too soon to go to the bar, but she was happy to stroll along in her new boots, her blister covered with new moleskin.

To her surprise, she came across a diner two blocks down the street. Where had that come from? Hadn't she asked…? She was beginning to wonder if anything Zeb Bowie said was true—including the story of his broken engagement. It could have been a line to gain her sympathy, though why he'd want that, she didn't know.

Like the bar, the place was right out of a Western movie, with a long Formica counter, checkered tablecloths, flowered curtains at the windows and the smell of coffee in the air. Chloe took a stool at the counter and looked around at the other late-afternoon customers—a solitary cowboy at the end of the counter and a couple at a table in the back—until the waitress approached with a green order pad in her hand.

"What'll you have, hon?" she asked.

"Coffee and a piece of that pie. Have you been here long?"

"Who, me?"

"I mean the diner."

"Only about thirty years."

"I see," Chloe said, seething inwardly. But there was no coffee shop in town, according to Zeb Bowie.

When the waitress brought her order, Chloe swallowed her anger and allowed herself to admire the towering meringue on the lemon pie. So much so she almost didn't notice the two men outside the window until the waitress waved to them. Her heart lurched. Even though she knew he was in town, she wasn't prepared to see Zeb Bowie yet. How *did* one prepare to see him? By straightening the shoulders. By taking a deep cleansing breath. By digging the toes of the boots into the floor. And clearing the throat so one could speak clearly without stumbling. Then curving the lips into a bland smile.

But there was no need to hurry. Because the two of them stood on the sidewalk waving their arms and talking in an animated manner to each other. As if she didn't exist. For all she knew they hadn't seen her; they were so engrossed in their conversation. She strained to hear their words or to read their lips, but finally gave up and turned to her pie and coffee.

"The Bowie brothers," the waitress said with a nod in their direction, as if that explained everything.

"Oh, yes. I've heard about them," Chloe said casually.

"Who hasn't?" the waitress asked. "Actually they're not as wild as they used to be. You know, the detergent in the fountain on the square that foamed all over the streets. And riding their horses backwards down Main Street in the May Day Parade."

Chloe shook her head in mock despair. "I suppose they come in to the diner from time to time," she said casually.

"All the time. Whenever they're in town. Everyone does. It may be Margie's pie or it may be the coffee. But sooner or later, everybody comes to the diner.''

Chloe glanced out the window and caught Zeb's eye. The liar. The unprincipled, unscrupulous liar. He waved, but he didn't come in.

''That's her?'' Sam asked. ''You never said she was young.''

''You didn't ask,'' Zeb said.

''Or that she was pretty,'' Sam said pressing his forehead against the window for a better look.

''It doesn't matter if she's Miss U.S.A. We have to have that land. Horatio would want us to have it,'' Zeb said.

''Then why didn't he leave it to us?'' Sam asked.

''Probably thought we didn't need it or want it. Which was true at the time. Before the anthrax epidemic and the flood. Now there's the dam,'' Zeb said. ''It's a whole new ball game. A new opportunity to save our hides. And those of our herd.''

''So what's the plan?'' Sam asked.

''We stick to her like glue. Don't let anybody get close enough to spill the beans. Once she finds out, we're sunk. We haven't got a chance. Not only will she refuse to sell the land…''

''She'll have a bad opinion of us,'' Sam suggested.

''To say the least,'' Zeb said grimly.

''Do you care?'' his brother asked with a curious glance.

''I don't particularly like being despised,'' Zeb said dryly.

"Yeah, I can see that. I can also see that waitress talking to her."

"What?" Zeb said. "Get in there."

"Me? What about you?" his brother asked.

"Both of us. One on each side of her."

Zeb pushed the door open. Chloe swiveled on her stool.

"Why, hello," he said, feigning surprise. "If it isn't my next-door neighbor." He slid smoothly onto the stool next to her. "Chloe, meet my brother Sam."

Sam shook her hand and sat on the other side of her. She turned her head from side to side, carefully studying both men. "Yes, I see the family resemblance," she said at last. "The same grizzled chin. The same bowed legs."

"Now, wait just a darn minute," Sam protested. "I'm a lot better looking than he is. And my legs aren't bowed."

"Relax, Sam. It's just a joke. Ms. Hudson here is just getting back at me for something I might have said." After a glance at Chloe's plate, both he and Sam ordered coffee and pie, too.

"The waitress and I were just talking about you," she said, picking up her coffee cup.

Zeb shot Sam a worried look over Chloe's head. "What about?" he asked.

"About the pranks you two used to play. And about the fact that this coffee shop has been here for thirty years and yet when you knew I was dying for a cup of coffee the other day, you didn't seem to know it existed."

"Of course I knew it existed. But you asked for a

coffee shop. This is a diner," he said smugly. "Isn't it, Mary Lou?" he asked the waitress, who was standing with her hands on her hips shaking her head at them. But she couldn't deny it.

"So what brings you to town this evening?" Zeb asked Chloe, admiring her profile while she ate her pie. The curve of her cheek, the straight nose, the stubborn chin. It was the stubborn chin that worried him.

"Same thing that brings you to town," she answered.

"Buying farm equipment?" Zeb asked, noticing a stray curl brush her smooth cheek. He squeezed his fork tightly in his hand to keep from reaching out to tuck that silky tendril behind her ear.

"Going to the bar for the steak dinner and the music," she said.

"Oh, that," he said. "I wouldn't bother if I were you. Besides, it might rain tonight and you wouldn't want to be caught on the trail in a downpour."

"Wait," Sam interrupted. "We can give her a ride home."

Zeb shot him a murderous glance.

"Can't we?" his brother asked innocently.

"If we're *going* home," Zeb said between clenched teeth. "Our plans are up in the air. If we go home at all, it might be very late. Or we might not be alone."

Chloe looked startled for just a moment, but she recovered with a quick smile. "I understand. After all, you've got your reputation to consider. What would people say if the Bowie brothers went home alone or too early? I wouldn't want to cramp your style. Or impose on you. I'm sure it's not going to rain, but if it does..." She held out one foot. "I've got new boots. Waterproof."

Zeb's spirits fell. Boots. She had waterproof boots. He should never have let her out of his sight. He should have been there every moment, to discourage her, to warn her and to hinder her efforts. Now she'd gone and bought these boots. Expensive boots, too, from the look of them.

"Well, we'd better be getting over to the bar, fire up those barbecue pits," Zeb said, draining his coffee cup and laying some bills on the counter.

Chloe did the same. "I'll walk over with you. Maybe I can be of some help."

"Oh, no," Sam said. "You're a customer."

Zeb shook his head at his brother as they walked three abreast along the narrow sidewalk.

"I mean, not unless you want to," Sam amended.

"She wants to," Zeb said, thinking she'd be better off in the kitchen where no random customer would strike up a conversation with her. "She's a great cook."

Chloe glanced up at Zeb, her gaze dubious, as if she doubted his sincerity. He met her gaze without wavering. It was one of the few truthful things he'd said to her or about her. She must have sensed it, because an energy flowed between them. And sparks flew. Right there on the sidewalk of the town of Powderkeg. He couldn't look away. Neither could she.

Sam was talking about something, but Zeb wasn't listening. He was listening to the voice in his head. The one that said, *This woman has your number. Don't lie to her, don't try to fool her. She's on to you. And sooner or later she'll make you pay for those lies.* He jerked his eyes from hers, told the voice in his head to shut up, and focused on the hills in the distance.

"Will any of your girlfriends be there tonight?" she asked.

"What girlfriends?" he asked. Lord, she could be annoying. What business was it of hers?

"You said you went out with women. They didn't get serious. Neither did you. Worked out fine. I thought they might be there tonight."

Exasperated, he exhaled loudly. "You have a memory like an elephant," he said. "I don't know who will be there. And I don't really care as long as they buy a steak and eat it. And recommend Bar Z meat to their friends. Here we are." He turned abruptly into the swinging front doors to the bar with his brother and Chloe close behind.

Barney was in the kitchen on a stepladder, taking plates off the top shelf of the cabinet when they trooped in. "Sam, Zeb, thank God you're here. I've got reservations up the kazoo. I hope to heaven you brought a lot of meat. I just wonder... Oh, hello, Ms. Hudson. Sorry about the mess." He looked around the small room at mesh bags of baking potatoes, slabs of butter and tubs of sour cream and shook his head. "Well, don't just stand there," he said to Zeb. "Do something. We've got about a hundred people coming here in an hour."

Stunned, Zeb looked at Sam and Sam looked at Barney.

"That's good," Zeb said at last. "I'll unload the meat from my truck."

"I'll light the charcoal," Sam said, heading out the door to the grill made from a fifty-gallon steel drum.

At the door Zeb stopped and turned to Barney. "Chloe wants to help. Give her an assignment."

But Barney was paralyzed. Incapable of giving anyone an assignment. "I should never have done this," he told Chloe as he climbed down from the stepladder when the brothers had left. "I became a bartender in a small town so I could take it easy. I don't need this kind of stress in my life. And I don't need more than twenty people in the bar at once. This was all Zeb's crazy idea. To sell his meat. To provide entertainment while people ate his meat." He pressed his hands to his temples.

"What's on the menu besides steak?" Chloe asked.

"Menu? There is no menu," Barney said, with a glazed look in his eyes.

"I mean what are you serving besides steak. Baked potatoes?"

"And salad," Barney said, and went into the bar to answer the telephone, still holding his head in his hands.

Chloe hesitated only a moment, then wrapped the potatoes in foil, neatly and efficiently, all one hundred of them, stacked them in the oven to bake at 350°. Then she opened the refrigerator and four huge bags of lettuce fell out. "There's the salad," she murmured to herself. "But where's the dressing?" The answer was there was no dressing. There were, however, bottles of oil and vinegar, a jar of Dijon mustard and salt and pepper. She whisked, she blended, she tasted and she cleaned up the kitchen. Leaving the potatoes behind to do their baking, she went out the back door to find the Bowie brothers bending over the smoking charcoal.

"You should have used lighter fluid," Zeb said, holding the can in his hand.

"What, and have the meat taste like chemicals?" Sam asked.

"Well, it's not going to taste like anything, because it's going to be raw."

"Give it a chance. You're so damned impatient," Sam said, pushing his brother away from the smoldering fire with a sooty hand.

Zeb's eyes glowed like angry, red-hot charcoal, and his polo shirt was covered with black soot. "I'm impatient? You think I'm impatient? Wait till you see all those people who have paid twelve dollars waiting for their steaks while you're back here staring at those coals. You're going to have a riot on your hands. And I'm not going to be here to protect you."

"Since when do I need you to protect me?" Sam asked indignantly, blowing on the coals.

"Since you were ten years old and Rick Russell stole your lunch on the school bus," Zeb said, fanning the coals from the other side.

"I didn't need you. You butted in, as usual. I had everything under control then, and I have everything under control now. So butt out."

Chloe watched horrified as Zeb menacingly raised his fist in the direction of Sam's chin.

"No," she shouted. "Stop."

Zeb dropped his arm and Sam looked up with a guilty start.

"See?" Sam said. "You've scared Chloe."

Zeb snorted. "You don't know her. She doesn't scare that easily."

"Do you two always fight like that?" she asked.

"Only when he does something stupid," Zeb explained. "Which is fairly frequent."

"Or when he thinks he knows everything, which is all the time," Sam said.

"Don't you fight with your sister or brother?" Zeb asked.

"No."

"That's too bad," Zeb said, watching his brother adjust the height of the grill. "Fighting with siblings helps you get along in the real world."

"Yes, I can see what I've missed out on," she said with a touch of sarcasm.

"Maybe we could adopt her," Sam suggested. "Isn't she just the kind of little sister you've always wanted?" He put one arm around Chloe, leaving dark smudge marks on her shirt.

"Great. That's all we need—is another mouth to feed. *You* adopt her, I'm going out in front to set up tables." And Zeb stomped through the kitchen and out into the bar.

"Don't mind him," Sam said going back to the grill. "He's not a bad guy really. I wouldn't tell him this, but he's actually protected me on more than one occasion. We've been in some tough spots together. On the ranch. In town. He yells and shouts, but underneath he's calm. Never really loses his cool. Right now he's a tad worried. Got a lot on his mind."

"One hundred steaks doesn't seem like that much to worry about," Chloe said.

"Other things too," Sam said. "Like money."

"Money? He offered to buy my property from me. He must have money."

"Oh, right. He'd, I mean *we'd* borrow the money from the bank."

"But why do you want the property?" Finally a chance to get a straight answer. Zeb's brother might be more forthcoming than he was. But then anybody might be more forthcoming than Zeb Bowie.

"Why?" Sam frowned. "Well, that's obvious, isn't it?"

"No, it isn't. I don't get it. A run-down hot-springs resort?"

"Why do *you* want it?" Sam asked.

"Because, because…it's complicated. Because it belonged to my great-grandfather, it's a part of my past. And because it's going to be my future."

"Your future?" he asked. "Your future what?"

"You won't laugh?" she asked.

He shook his head.

"He didn't tell you?"

"No."

"I'm going to turn it into a health spa." Chloe held her breath. If anyone else laughed at her idea she didn't think she could take it. It was hard enough keeping the faith when she looked around at that old swimming pool and the decrepit cabins, but to have another Bowie brother laugh at her dream would be the last straw.

He didn't laugh. He just nodded. "That's an interesting idea," he said.

"Thank you," she said with a sigh of relief. Before he could ask any questions like, 'How are you going to do *that?*' she went back to the kitchen to check on the potatoes.

Where she ran into Zeb. Literally ran into him, and had the breath knocked out of her. She bounced off his broad chest and washboard stomach, staggered backwards and leaned against the counter, breathing hard, studying the rugged man who never lost his cool, and had a lot on his mind.

"Careful," he said, reaching out to rub a smudge off her shirt, his hand lingering on the full curve of her breast.

"What are you doing?" she asked in a shaky voice.

"Isn't it obvious?" he asked, his fingers making concentric circles around her nipples. "I'm cleaning your shirt for you."

The kitchen was hot. The potatoes were roasting. Chloe couldn't have been any warmer if she'd been roasting right along with them. Not only that but there was no air in there. No air for her to breathe. Her breasts were so full, so heavy with desire. Where did this come from, this sudden flood of sexual desire in the middle of a small kitchen?

It wasn't the oven heating her up. It was his steady gaze and the touch of his work-roughened hands that made her cheeks flame and her body throb with longing. *Wasn't it obvious,* he wanted to know. Yes, it was obvious he was there to drive her crazy with unfulfilled desire. Not that it could ever be fulfilled. Not with a playboy like him.

She stepped back. "No problem. Everything's

washable," she said a trifle unsteadily. "The shirt…me."

"I'll help you wash up," he said with a gleam in his eye. "The shirt…you."

Help her wash up? She could just imagine his wet, soapy hands cupping her heavy breasts, then moving to her sensitive nipples. She stifled a moan in the back of her throat. They were in the commercial kitchen of the town bar and she was fantasizing about making love to a notorious ladies' man. What had happened to the crisp, efficient nurse who had everything, including herself, under control?

"That…that won't be necessary," she said straightening her shoulders, and rubbing her hands on her jeans. "Well, everything's under control here," she lied, trying to stop her hands from shaking and her knees from wobbling. "What else can we do?"

"I can think of a lot of things," he said, a devilish, sexy grin creasing his face. "But they'll have to wait till after dinner."

Six

After she and Barney had served one-hundred-plus sizzling steaks, each flanked by a fluffy baked potato and a crisp salad, Chloe sank into a chair in the corner of the crowded bar to listen to the three-piece blues band Barney had hired. Which was a mistake. The plaintive lyrics of "Blues, Leave Me Alone" went straight to her heart, reminding her that love doesn't last. The moody bass guitar reverberated through her, making her remember how it felt to be lost and alone and betrayed. She was too tired to eat, too tired to think. All she could do was feel. And what she felt was sad and blue. Just as well she couldn't think, because if she could, she might think about Zeb Bowie and the promise of seduction in his brilliant blue eyes.

If he came on to her now, when she was so tired,

so defenseless, filled not with food, but with longing for something she couldn't have, she didn't know how she'd resist. On top of everything else, there was the music. Sad songs full of melancholy, of tears and parting. Enough to break down the defenses of a tower of strength—which she certainly was not.

She reminded herself that Zeb wasn't going to come on to her. There were plenty of attractive women in the bar at this moment, she noted and some of them were probably his girlfriends, past, present or future.

What if she slipped out now, got into her car and headed for home? No one would miss her. Or would they? It was clear Barney and the Bowies were overwhelmed by their success. So overwhelmed they didn't have enough help either to serve the dinner or clean up afterward. They might be counting on her. They certainly needed her.

She started to stand, then felt a large, firm hand on her shoulder, pushing her back down in her chair. Zeb eased himself into the chair next to hers. "Enjoying the music?" he said under his breath so as not to disturb the trio. He was so close she could feel his warm breath against her ear. His shoulder was pressed against hers. Her bones seemed to have turned to jelly. She might not be able to get up and go anywhere. Any time.

She nodded. "Is it time to clean up?" she whispered back.

"It's done. Barney hired a couple of teenagers. I've got my truck packed up. Want to leave?" He held out his hand.

She took it and let him pull her to her feet. The

band was now playing "Blues Before Sunrise." It was time to get out of there.

"I'll walk you to your car," he said as he guided her out the front door, still holding her hand tightly. "You know," he said as they walked down the quiet street past stores long since shut down for the night, "we could pick you up at the Paradise Springs entrance where you park your car and give you a ride to your property line. Save you a long walk in."

"No thanks," she said, picturing sharing the front seat with his date for the evening. "I'll enjoy a little hike this time of night." A hike in the dark, where roots and branches reached out to snare her ankle or hit her on the head. Where wild bears hid behind trees just waiting to pounce on her. Sure she would. But all that was better than blues before sunrise. "You're not going home alone, are you?" she asked pointedly.

"No," he said brusquely. But he figured Sam wouldn't mind giving her a lift, too. "I'm going home with Sam."

"Uh-huh." Just as she supposed. Well, she wouldn't be a party to his little games.

He dropped her hand. "So you won't take a ride?"

"If Great-Grandpa Horatio could walk that trail at age eighty-seven, I can too." She unlocked her car door. "Thanks anyway."

He leaned down and spoke to her through the side window. "Thanks for helping out. I..." he said.

She turned the key in the ignition. She didn't want to prolong this goodbye, didn't want him elaborating on his previous suggestion—that he could think of a lot of things they could do. So could she. She had to

get out of there before he said something, did something and she found herself saying something or doing something she'd be sorry for later.

She pulled away in her car while he was still talking. When she glanced in her rearview mirror, she
saw him standing in the middle of Main Street with
his arms across his chest watching her leave town.
Maybe no one had ever left him in the middle of a
sentence like that. If not, it was about time somebody
did.

"What did she say when you asked her?" Sam
asked as they drove down the highway on their way
home.

"Said she'd enjoy a hike. Said if her grandpa
could walk that trail, then so could she."

"Got a lot of spunk," Sam remarked.

"Yeah. Like her grandpa," Zeb said.

"Anything going on between you two?" Sam
asked.

"Absolutely not. Wouldn't be right," Zeb said.

"Wouldn't be fair," Sam added. "So you
wouldn't mind if I…?"

"Try it and I'll break your face in half."

"That's what I thought," Sam said with a knowing smirk.

"Let me off at the Paradise Springs entrance,"
Zeb said.

Sam gave him an inquisitive look, but he didn't
say anything. Good thing he didn't ask any questions, because Zeb didn't have any answers. He just
knew he had to catch up with Chloe. That there was
unfinished business between them. For one thing, he

hadn't thanked her properly for all the work she'd done that night.

All the while she'd been frantically busy barbecuing steaks, he couldn't shake the image of her in the kitchen, her heat-flushed face, her luminous eyes, the way she held her breath when he caressed her breasts, the way they seemed to swell to fit his hands. Just thinking about her now made him go rigid with need.

"Can't you drive any faster?" he demanded through clenched teeth.

"I'm going sixty-five," Sam said mildly with a quick glance at his brother. "How're you gonna catch her anyway? She's miles ahead of us. Probably halfway home by now."

"Let me worry about that," Zeb said.

Ten minutes later Sam let Zeb out at the trailhead. He glanced over his shoulder to watch the lights of the truck disappear in the darkness. And instantly regretted this stupid, ill-conceived plan. He didn't even have a flashlight. He was a fool. He'd been even more of a fool to think he could put Chloe out of his mind by staying away from Paradise Springs these past few days. He ran into her in the diner and bang, she wove her spell around him just like she had the first day she arrived. That's what it was, it was a magic spell. Because no ordinary woman had this kind of power over him. Not even Joanne. He didn't like it. Not one bit. He was going to exorcise that spell tonight, or he'd turn in his membership card to the Bowie Brothers Wild Man Club. The Bowie Brothers never let a woman have the last word. Never let them have the upper hand.

So what was he doing, pursuing a woman down a dark, overgrown trail in the middle of the night, he asked himself as he recklessly splashed through a small stream. Usually they pursued him. But where the hell was she?

"Chloe," he shouted. "Chloe, stop. Wait for me."

No answer. The forest was still except for the hooting of an owl, the occasional sound of a deer or a raccoon crashing through the brush. Or could it be a *woman* crashing through the brush, a woman who didn't want to see him or talk to him? She was so damned stubborn. Who knew what she wanted or why she wanted it? Sometimes she seemed responsive to his advances, other times she brushed him off like an annoying deer tick.

"Chloe," he yelled. "Where are you?"

He thought he heard a voice. He plunged forward, the branches tearing at his clothes. His eyes were finally accustomed to the dark, but in his haste he still stumbled and tripped on fallen limbs and unexpected rocks.

It *was* a voice. It was her voice. Very small and far away. But it kept him going. Until he found her sitting on a boulder on the side of the trail, calmly watching him frantically climb up to join her. As if she knew he'd come. As if this was some midsummer picnic instead of a late-night chase through the darkness.

Instead of throwing her arms around him and heaving a sigh of relief at being rescued, she surveyed him coolly. "What are you doing here?" she asked.

"I was worried about you. I told you I wanted to walk you home."

She hopped off the boulder and continued the upward climb to the springs. "You also told me you wouldn't be going home alone, that your plans were up in the air. I certainly wouldn't want to cramp your style."

"So that's what this is all about. You're jealous," he said, smiling to himself in the dark.

She whirled around and confronted him. "Jealous? I'm jealous? Of who?"

"Of my past, of the legions of women in my life."

"Oh, right," she said. "If anyone's jealous, it's you. You're jealous of my land, aren't you? Of my ability to adapt to the Wild West." She turned on the heel of her new waterproof boot and continued marching up the trail, the beam from her flashlight illuminating the trail ahead of her.

He saved his answer until they reached the tumbledown resort, inhaled the faint smell of minerals in the air, saw the ever-present plume of steam outlined against the dark sky.

"Okay," he said, noting with satisfaction that when they reached the clearing in front of the bathhouse she was breathing hard. "I *am* jealous of your land. I haven't made a secret of the fact that I want it. Say the word and I'll give you a fair price for it."

"Never," she said, leaning against a spruce tree.

He shrugged. This was not the time to press her. Not when she was in this feisty mood. But then, when wasn't she? "I'm not jealous of your adapting to the Wild West. I'm impressed. I didn't give you enough credit. You've managed to survive here in the wilds with no amenities. I'm…what can I say? I'm amazed at your fortitude, your stick-to-itiveness, your hard work."

"That's enough flattery," she said "I'm not going to sell you the land."

He crossed the clearing, stepping over piles of brush, and put his hands on her shoulders. "Forget the land for one damn minute. Can't you tell the difference between flattery and honesty?" he asked. "Don't you feel proud of yourself for what you've done here?" He gestured to the brush piles, to the ground she'd cleared. "If you're not, I am. When I first saw you I wouldn't have given you twenty-four hours here. Do you have any idea how I feel about you," he blurted. "Besides proud?"

Speechless with surprise at his outburst, she shook her head.

"I don't either," he confessed. "So that makes two of us."

A gurgle of laughter escaped from her throat. She shook her head. "At least you're honest."

Honest? Oh, lord, if she only knew. For one crazy moment he almost told her the truth. The whole story. It was the way she looked at him, with a combination of trust, amusement and downright anticipation that tempted him to confess. Then a smile curved her lips and he squashed the idea of taking the honesty route. He couldn't stand to see that smile fade.

A gleam shone in her dark eyes, an awareness of highly charged particles in the air, of the tension that was always there between them. In the diner, at the bar, out in the open. Everywhere, it was always there and always building. One of these days or one of these nights, it was going to snap like a rubber band that was stretched too tight. Was this the night? The night for passion? For lust, pure and simple? He knew the answer. It was yes, yes and yes. Was it the night for honesty? No. Honesty would just muck things up. Probably for good.

She lifted her hand to his face and traced the hard line of his jaw with her finger.

Her touch was so soft, so gentle, yet so unmistakably inviting. "Oh, sweetheart," he breathed. "I hope you know what you're doing."

The answer was there in her eyes. She knew, she knew. She lifted her lips to his. He would have been crazy to ignore the invitation And Mrs. Bowie didn't raise any crazy children.

He took her mouth completely in one swift motion. He was tired of wondering. Tired of flirting. And talking. He wanted her. All of her. Now. Their tongues tangled in a rapturous kiss that went on and on and made his heart hammer until she finally came up for air.

Chloe clung to him, her arms around his neck, her body pressed against his, merging with his until she was desperate to feel the texture of his skin and the heat from his body without clothing in the way. He picked her up with one swift motion, and carried her to the bathhouse. She dug her face into his neck, nuzzling and kissing him as he kicked the door open and set her on the bench.

Dazed and dizzy, Chloe watched Zeb turn on the hot water to fill the tub. Her body was aching, throbbing with desire. She needed him, wanted him. She had reason to think he felt the same. Through the steam she watched Zeb come toward her, his eyes burning.

"Brings back memories," he said, watching her with the same heated gaze he'd fixed on her that very first day. "I wanted to take your clothes off then and I want to now." He knelt next to the bench and unbuttoned her shirt, his fingers clumsy and awkward.

Impatient, she yanked her shirt over her head, unsnapped her bra and tossed it aside. Finally her breasts, swollen with lust and longing, were free. Zeb didn't move, didn't speak. He just stared at her as if she were a statue just unveiled for his pleasure. Maybe he thought she was wanton. Maybe he thought she had no scruples. Maybe he'd regret this tomorrow. Maybe she would, too. But at the moment she didn't care. She needed this. Now. She needed him. Now. To feel whole again. To feel wanted, desired again.

"My God, Chloe, you're so...so beautiful," he stammered. He reached for her then and cradled her breasts in his hands. She felt her nipples peak as he stroked them reverently with the pads of his thumbs. Her body quivered, every cell, every pore alive and aware.

Arching her body to give him access, she suddenly glimpsed the water cresting over the top of the tub. "Zeb, the water," she gasped.

He let some out, then motioned for her to get in. She approached cautiously, watching him kick off his shoes and strip down to his jeans.

"I want you to come in, too," she said, in a

breathy voice she hardly recognized. She quickly shed the rest of her clothes.

"I'm coming all right, sweetheart," he promised, ripping his jeans off as he watched her slip into the tub.

She wanted a good look at him, at his body in all its naked magnificence, but he slid into the water before she could satisfy her curiosity. With his hands on her shoulders, he held her on top of him, her back against his chest, where she half floated, half rested, half satisfied, half frustrated, as his arms went around her. His broad fingers stroked the outline of her breasts, then moved to her belly and the soft slick skin of her inner thighs. She shuddered. A rush of pure sexual desire left her quivering, begging for release. She was losing control fast, too fast.

She wanted to see him, touch him, and feel him go rigid at her touch. She twisted around to face him, reached for the soap, and started a lazy journey down his body. Her hands traveled from his broad shoulders to his chest to his navel, reveling in the rise and fall of his chest, in the heavy thudding of his heart. In the sounds he made, all male, all macho groans of pleasure and of protest.

"Chloe, hell, what are you...oh, yes, yes...," he said as her soapy hands stroked his rigid masculinity.

Stunned by the strength of his response, she felt excitement fluttering in her very core. Excitement and need and wonder at the size of him. Her breath was coming in short gasps now as she realized how hot and how wet and ready she was. How ready he was. How close they were to the point of no return. Not that she wanted to return. She wanted to move ahead. To close the gap between them. Once and forever.

With a deep hoarse sound, he gripped her shoulders and thrust upward, filling her as she'd never been filled before. Her body was hot and wet and slick as his strong, demanding thrusts drove her higher and higher onto another level of consciousness. Until the painful pleasure peaked, and in one dizzying moment she went over the edge. She called his name. He shouted hers.

His eyes were closed, his lips pressed together in a sublime smile. He was drifting...no, he was sinking.

"Zeb," she said, alarmed, pulling his head up out of the water. "You're drowning."

"I don't care," he said and he meant it. He could die right now a happy man. On the other hand, if he stayed alive, he might live to do this all over again.

"Come here," he said. He sat up and, with his hands on her temples brought her mouth to meet his.

He brushed his lips across hers, tangling his hands in her wet curls possessively. He wondered for the nth time how any man could have ever let her go. She was everything a man could want— generous, warm, loving, lovable. It took all his self-control to remind himself not to get involved with another woman. Especially one who didn't fit in here. No matter how lovable she was.

In fact, the more lovable, warm and generous she was, the more likely she was to be desired by someone else. And the more likely to go off with someone else when his back was turned. He'd never forget the pain and humiliation he'd felt when Joanne left. How his friends had looked at him, with a mixture of pity and astonishment at his stupidity.

This was a different matter. This was a one-night stand, or maybe two or three. As long as she was willing. As long as she never knew he wanted her land more than he wanted her. Needed her land for his own survival. If he played his cards right, she'd never find out. But if she did... He shuddered to think what she'd think.

If he'd met her sooner, it might have been a different story. Before he was disillusioned about women. Before she was disillusioned about men. Before he'd decided that women couldn't be relied on. Before she'd decided that men couldn't be trusted.

As if she'd read his mind, and suddenly saw how conniving and devious he was, she drew back and studied his face for a long moment. He didn't know what she saw there, but whatever it was, she stepped out of the tub and wrapped a large towel around her, knotting it above her breasts.

"So now what?" she asked briskly, as if they'd just finished a hand of poker.

He followed her out of the tub, dripping water across the floor and braced one arm against the wall. "I was thinking about spending the night in your hammock, with you," he said. He'd been thinking about it since the day she'd bought it. Thinking about sleeping next to her in it, her body folded tight against his, one hand stroking those beautiful breasts, the other sliding between her legs to find that secret spot, to bring her to another climax and another and another... Then he remembered he'd already sug-

gested a night in her hammock the last time he'd
been there and she'd turned him down flat. Something about not wanting to fulfill her romantic fantasy. Not with him, anyway.

Whatever the reason, she had the same look on
her face as last time, the look that said, *I don't think
so.* He couldn't take being turned down again, not
after what had just happened. Not after that earthshaking experience in the tub. It had left him feeling
like an overcharged battery, or as if his head were
floating above his body, looking down at him. That
could be due to his extended immersion in hot water—or it could be something else.

Damn...his blood pumped just remembering how
she floated on top of him, the water lapping against
her rosebud nipples. A fever raged somewhere inside
him. He grabbed a towel to wrap around his waist
and hide his throbbing erection. No, he couldn't
chance a rejection. The best thing was to pretend his
suggestion had been a joke.

"I was thinking about the hammock," he continued. "But on second thought it's probably not big
enough for two and you've probably got other plans
for the night, like sleeping." There, that ought to let
her off the hook. He forced a smile, grabbed his
clothes and went out in the night air, hoping it would
cool more than his head.

When she came out, still wrapped in the towel,
looking puzzled and dazed, a shaft of guilt struck him
between his ribs. Obviously, he shouldn't have said
what he'd said, or she wouldn't have that look on
her face. Ladies' man that he was, or was alleged to

be, he still didn't know what you were supposed to say on an occasion like this. "Thanks for a wonderful evening" didn't seem to cut it. "We'll have to do it again sometime" seemed presumptuous. So he didn't say anything except "Good night." She didn't say anything at all. So he raised his hand in a casual gesture and took off, feeling like a total jerk. A guilty jerk.

Chloe stood barefoot, wrapped only in her towel, staring off in the direction of the Bar Z Ranch long after the sound of Zeb's footsteps had faded in the darkness. She stood there until a chill came over her, so intense that she started to shake uncontrollably. Yes, she knew he'd leave. No, she didn't want him to stay. Yes, she knew what he wanted from her. Her land. And her body. In that order.

He'd been honest about that. He'd been honest about everything. No sweet talk. No flattery. Except to say he admired her for her hard work. Since he couldn't have her land, and she thought she'd made that perfectly clear, then he wanted a night of fun with her.

She knew what she wanted from him, too. And she'd gotten it. One evening of ecstasy unlike any she'd ever known before or would likely ever know again. She threw on a pair of sweat pants and a sweat shirt, wrapped herself in a thick blanket and lay down in her hammock. Still cold and still alone. "Blues, leave me alone," she muttered.

After all, what had she expected? That he'd spend the night with her? Holding her? Protecting her from

wild animals and her fears of failure and loss and of
being deserted? No, he couldn't get out of there fast
enough. Probably afraid she'd burst into tears or demand a dozen roses and a thank-you note. Men like
him didn't spend the night. Men like him didn't make
promises they couldn't keep or send flowers the next
day. So what?

He'd said he had no idea how he felt about her.
But she knew exactly how she felt about him. He
alternately amused her, surprised her and irritated
her. And he always always attracted her. Like a bee
to honey. Like iron to a magnet. Despite her best
intentions, she couldn't stay away from him. In the
water or out of it. Damn him. She'd come here with
the firm intention of avoiding another disastrous romantic entanglement with a man, any man. But especially one with a roving eye. One who had no intention of settling down with one woman.

And what had happened? She'd been here a little
over a week and already she was in hot water. Literally. Which didn't mean she had to stay in hot water. Not with him, anyway. She could get along without Zeb Bowie. She could make this place a success
on her own. On Monday morning she was going to
take steps in that direction.

Restless, she got out of the hammock, went to the
cabin she'd cleaned and modestly furnished with an
inflatable mattress, and lit the gas lantern. Sitting on
the edge of the mattress, she made a shopping list:

1. electric power lines
2. telephone lines

3. a road
4. a kitchen and dining room

She didn't know how much power lines cost, but it couldn't be cheap to bring them in all this way, especially without a road. Ditto telephone lines. She opened her bankbook and stared at the numbers. How naive she'd been to think her divorce settlement, as generous as it was, would begin to cover the cost of converting this old resort into a spa. It was going to take money. Lots of money. But the end result was going to be nothing less than spectacular. Rustic, but luxurious. Natural, yet comfortable. Thinking about the spa helped her forget Zeb Bowie and shake the lingering feeling that tonight had been a terrible mistake.

She forced herself to think about a dining room with a view of the mountains, featuring delicious, low-calorie food. She made herself imagine the women riding horses or hiking or just swinging in hammocks, sipping mineral water after a massage and a facial. After her divorce, her mother had treated her to a spa visit and she remembered how the tension had oozed out of her body, and left her feeling refreshed and revived. If she could do that for other women, she'd feel she'd accomplished something. Of course she accomplished something every day as a nurse, but when she was promoted, she'd found herself doing more and more administrative work, while the hard, but satisfying patient care was left to aides.

She tore a new sheet of paper from the pad and began sketching buildings, inside and out, making a rough map of her property based on her tour on horseback. By the time she'd finished she had a whole sheaf of papers. Papers that would, *should* impress the local banker enough to get a loan.

Seven

———

Zeb shaded his eyes against the dazzling morning sunshine as he walked in the direction of the back pasture. Another sleepless night. He used to sleep like a rock. But that was B.C. Before Chloe. Before she came along and threw his life into chaos. Took away his hot tub, threatened his dream of buying her property, and worst of all, made him want what he couldn't have. Her.

Last night as he lay in his bed, the sheets twisted around his legs, hot, restless and frustrated, he'd replayed the scene in the hot tub over and over. Wondering why he hadn't spent the night, woken up in her hammock with her in the morning, the scent of her hair filling his senses, her soft, warm curves filling his arms. Wondering what he'd done wrong. What he'd said wrong.

He found his brother leaning against the fence watching the cows graze. The peaceful scene usually calmed Zeb's nerves. Today the sight of all those fertile cows and no bull made him edgy and depressed. Silently he joined his brother to gaze moodily at the green pasture.

"Didn't hear you come in last night," Sam said, chewing on a stalk of grass. "Was it late?"

"No."

"Why not?"

"Why not? Because she...because I..." He ran his hand through his hair. "Hell, I don't know."

"Did you make any progress?"

Zeb gave his brother a long, hard look.

"Toward getting the land," Sam explained.

"Oh, that."

"Yes, that. Isn't that why you followed her home, to talk her out of the land?" Sam asked.

"Yeah, sure." Sam was right. He was losing sight of his objective. "No, the answer is no. Not only did I not make any progress, I think I lost some ground. The harder I try to convince her she doesn't belong here, the more determined she is to stay."

"She has a stubborn streak," Sam said. "I could see it in her chin. Maybe we ought to try some reverse psychology. Tell her to stay. Help her out a little."

"Help her out a little? I've done nothing but help her out since the day she arrived. Took her on a tour of the property by horseback, gave her a ride to town, carried her supplies in for her. What more does she want?" Zeb demanded.

"She wants to build a spa on her property," Sam said.

"Well I'm not going to help her build her spa. That's the worst idea I ever heard. Old Horatio must be twirling in his grave. Let's forget Chloe for a moment, can we?" he asked.

"I can," Sam said, "but can you? You're the one who's been talking about her nonstop since she got here."

"All right. Fine. Not another word about her. I'm sick of waiting for her to come around. We need money now. Money for the bull. I'm going in to see Archie at the bank for another loan."

"I thought he said he wouldn't lend us any more."

"I've got to try. How much do we need?"

Sam filled him in on the various bulls he had seen for sale and their prices and before he could lose his nerve, Zeb left to see the bank president, loan officer and owner, an old man who'd been there as long as the bank itself. Archibald Crane was as shrewd and tightfisted as they came. Zeb would rather have wrestled a bull to the ground than ask him for any more money, but he had no choice. Not that he was giving up on getting Paradise Springs. It was just going to take a little longer than he'd first thought. A little longer until *she* came to the inevitable conclusion that she didn't belong there.

Since their bull had died in the anthrax epidemic last year, he and Sam hadn't been able to do any breeding. And without breeding, they might as well close up shop and give up the land that had been in their family for all these years. He stared straight ahead as he drove into town, unable to look at the neatly fenced green fields on either side of the road, without feeling jealousy of his neighbors' financial security. Not that he'd trade the Bar Z for any other ranch. He just wanted to be out of debt. They were so close to that goal...so close, as close as their property line...and yet so far away. And it was all *her* fault.

"Archie in?" Zeb asked Mavis behind the teller's window.

"Think so. Go knock on his door," she suggested.

Crane was behind his desk, in his starched high-collar shirt, the same style he'd been wearing for the past fifty years, his head resting against the back of his leather chair, regarding Zeb with narrowed eyes.

"What now?" he asked.

Not a good beginning, but not unexpected either. "Good to see you, Archie. You're looking well." Zeb said..

"More than I can say for you. You look like you slept in your clothes. All wrinkled. Honest to God, I don't know what it is with you young people. If you can't dress proper when you come to town, you ought to stay home."

"I'd like to stay home, but as you know we've had a run of bad luck," Zeb said.

"Bad luck? People make their own luck," Archie said, gripping the lapels of his suit jacket with his thumb and forefinger.

"Arch, we had the anthrax epidemic and then the floods last spring. Not much we could have done about either."

"Maybe yes, maybe no. In any case, once they get

the dam built, won't have to worry any more about flooding.''

"Oh, yes, the dam," Zeb said as casually as he could. "Any word on that?"

"It's going through, from what I've heard. Lucky for you it won't touch your property. But Paradise Springs will be no more. Wouldn't Horatio have been surprised to hear that his property would be worth something, after all? At least his great-granddaughter will get something out of it. Guess that's why she came out. Wants to see the place before it goes under.''

"Oh, you heard about her?" Zeb asked, a sick, sinking feeling in the pit of his stomach. What if Archie ran into Chloe…no, not likely. At his age, Archie never went anywhere, except to the bank and home again. And considering the long walk down the trail, it would probably be a while before Chloe set foot in town again.

"Heard she's right pretty, that true?"

"I didn't notice."

"What's wrong with you, boy? How old are you, thirty-two, thirty-three? And still not married? How you going to carry on the Bowie line if you don't notice pretty women?"

Zeb ground his teeth in frustration. A week ago no one had heard of Horatio's great-granddaughter. Now he couldn't go anywhere, including his own pasture, without having to discuss her—her looks, her assets and her plans.

"You're right," Zeb said. "But first I need a bull."

The wrinkles in the old man's face deepened. "What?"

"If I'm going to propose to somebody, I've got to have something to offer her."

"Why?" Archie asked. "In my day it was the woman who brought her dowry to the table. Why don't you marry somebody with a bull?"

"That's a great idea. I just might do that. When I find someone. But for the moment..." He took a breath. "We need a loan to buy one of our own." There, it was out.

But Archie had started shaking his head before Zeb even got the words out of his mouth. He should have known. He did know. But he had to ask anyway. "Why not, Archie?" Zeb asked, standing before the man who could turn his fortunes around. "You won't miss the money and it will turn things around for us."

"You're up to your ears in debt now, boy," he said. "It would be irresponsible of me to lend you any more money. How would I explain it to the board of trustees?"

Zeb could hardly keep from pounding the desk in frustration. Everyone knew old Archie controlled the board of trustees with an iron fist. Anything he wanted from them, he got.

"And now," Archie said, taking out his gold pocket watch to check the time. "If you'll excuse me, it's lunchtime." As he spoke he reached under his desk for a wicker picnic hamper, took out a large checkered napkin, laid it on his desk, followed by a thermos of coffee, a half of a cold roast chicken and

a wedge of sharp cheddar cheese. Zeb salivated, remembering that he'd skipped breakfast that morning.

Zeb was about to protest, but after a glance at Archie with his mouth full of chicken, he turned and
went to the door. When he opened it, Chloe was
standing there, her hand in the air, poised to knock.
As he gripped the doorknob, his heart ricocheted in
his chest.

"Chloe," he said. "Uh...somebody else to see
you, Archie," Zeb said, holding the door open so
Chloe could hear the answer, loud and clear.

"Close the door," the old man bellowed. "It's
lunchtime."

Startled, Chloe stepped back. "Was that...the
bank president?"

"That was him. And I wouldn't advise disturbing
him during his lunch hour. Can I help?" he asked,
closing the door firmly behind him, and guiding her
past the lone teller out into the sunshine.

"I don't think so," she said. "I'm here to ask
about a loan."

Zeb shook his head. "You've come to the wrong
place. Archibald Crane doesn't loan money," he said
with a trace of bitterness. "At least not to people like
us who need it. It's his policy to lend money to people who already have money. I know, because he just
turned me down."

"I don't believe that. The teller said he was not
only the president of the bank, but the loan officer
as well."

"And the chairman of the board of trustees, the
owner and chief financial officer."

"Then I'm going to see him. If I have to wait all day."

"Tell you what I'm going to do," Zeb said, his mind racing a mile a minute. "While you're waiting, while he's having his lunch, I'm going to buy *you* lunch and coach you on what to say to Crane."

"Why would you do that?" she asked, studying him with her dark eyes. "You've done nothing but discourage me from the moment I arrived."

"I didn't realize how determined you were. How serious. I thought you were just playing around. Now I realize…" What, what did he realize? That he couldn't get her out of his mind. That her red-gold hair held glints of copper in the sun. That her eyes that could be meltingly soft one moment and as deep as dark, bittersweet chocolate the next. That she was blessed—or cursed—with gritty determination and a stubborn chin.

If he hadn't made love to her…then things would be different. He could walk away right now and never see her again. But if he hadn't made love to her he wouldn't have known how earthshaking love-making could be. But was it a fluke? Was it a once-in-a-lifetime experience that couldn't be, wouldn't be repeated? He was operating on that assumption. If he didn't, he might become obsessed by finding a way to repeat the experience.

He also realized that Chloe was not going quietly. That he couldn't keep her from going to town, and that every time she did, she was in danger of hearing about the dam. Archie would be the first one to tell her. If he didn't stop him.

"Now I realize how determined you are," he finished.

"I know. You said that," she said impatiently. "Where are we going to eat?"

A view of the diner at lunchtime flashed through his mind. Packed with people, any one of whom might say something about the dam.

"We're having a picnic," he announced. Which would be a real challenge, since there was no park in town and no deli where he could buy picnic food.

"I love picnics," Chloe said an hour later, leaning back against a red sandstone rock in the hills outside of town. She was hungry, ravenous, and salivating as she watched Zeb unwrap huge sandwiches of roast beef, cheese, peppers and lettuce and tomato and hand her one. She didn't know where he'd got them, and she didn't care. She'd gone shopping at the dry-goods store until he picked her up and brought her to this rock garden with its grove of ponderosa pine.

"I knew that," Zeb said, reaching into his bag to pull out potato chips and sodas and set them on the blanket between them.

"Did you also know I'd be at the bank this morning?" she asked between bites. "Isn't it strange how we're always running into each other?"

"Not that strange. It's a small town." He took a large bite of his sandwich and chewed thoughtfully. "I'm glad I ran into you. I never got a chance to thank you for last night."

"Thank me?" Chloe almost choked. He was going to thank her for making love with him. She could feel the heat rise to her head. Her cheeks flamed.

"For helping out with the steak dinners. We never could have done it..." He paused in mid-sentence. "Oh, you thought..." He shot her an almost bashful grin that turned his ears red. "No, that's not what I meant."

Then he stared off into space, making her wonder if he was having as hard a time as she was acting natural after what had happened last night. Maybe he was embarrassed, too. Maybe he was sorry it had happened.

"I don't know what you must have thought of me," she said, nervously ripping open a package of chips. "I don't usually...I don't ever."

"I'll tell you what I thought of you," he said, leaning forward across the blanket to look into her eyes. "I thought you were the most beautiful, the sexiest, the sweetest..."

Her gaze locked on his. She wanted to believe him. What woman wouldn't? But maybe he told every woman the same thing. No flowers, no promises, no thank-you notes. Just an overdose of flattery the next day. Well, she could give it as well as take it.

"You're a good-looking... I mean, you're pretty sexy yourself," she said. "I started to say that I don't usually do that kind of thing with a total stranger."

"Total stranger? Stranger, maybe, but not total. I thought we'd gotten beyond total," he said with a frown. "Especially after last night."

Again she blushed as she brushed a pine needle from her lap. "Okay, yes. Whatever we are, we can't be... I mean, we can't do that anymore."

"Why not?" he asked, so surprised she began to wonder why herself.

"Because I'm on the rebound. After being dumped by my husband, I'm just trying to prove I'm still desirable. It's not fair to you to use you this way."

"I don't mind," he said, barely suppressing his smile.

"I'm serious," she insisted. "And from what you told me about your fiancée, you may be in the same position."

"After two years? I don't think so."

Now it was her turn to smile. "You mean you have no doubts about how desirable you are?"

"Well..." He tried to look modest, but she could tell he was having a hard time. He knew damn well how sexy and appealing he was. He also knew why she'd made love to him. Despite what she'd said, it had nothing to do with her insecurity. It had everything to do with him. And the electricity between them. It was new to her, but perhaps he carried it around with him, setting off electrical charges wherever he went, whoever he went with.

"Back to the bank," she said.

"Already?"

"I mean the subject of the bank. What were you doing there, if I may ask."

"Same as you. To borrow money," he said.

"But you must have money. You want to buy my land."

"Oh, I do. I have money to buy your land. I just don't have money to buy a bull. Which I need very badly."

"I see," she said. But she didn't see at all. How much did bulls cost, anyway?

"Now," he said before she could ask another question. "When you go into the bank, you've got to be prepared. Let me tell you, I know what he's going to say. Let's go over the scenario. I'll be Archie, the bank president, you be you." Zeb sat up straight as a ramrod in a perfect imitation of the stern banker. "So you want to borrow money from the bank, young lady. What for?"

"For my spa."

"Spa?" he said gruffly. "What in hell is a spa?"

"A spa is a resort for women, or men, of course," she said earnestly, "who need a time and a place to rejuvenate themselves. In the country, preferably. Away from the bustle of the city. Where they can get back into shape, physically and mentally."

"How they going to do that, at that broken-down hot-springs resort?" Zeb asked.

"That's what I need the money for." She reached into her shoulder bag to pull out her plans and her lists and shoved them in Zeb's direction across the blanket.

He studied them briefly. Then he cleared his throat. "Road, buildings, power, telephone. Looks like you need a couple million to do all this."

Her face fell. He could be saying that to discourage her. But he could be right, too.

"But..."

"Here's what I tell folks like you, little lady..."

Chloe grimaced.

"I tell them to start small. Prove to me, and to my board of directors to whom I must account, that you can succeed in a small way first before you go for the big bucks."

"A small way? You mean a small spa?" she asked.

"No, no, no. Something else, that utilizes your natural resources, like…like…selling mineral water," Zeb said.

"From my springs."

"Exactly."

"But how, where, what…?" she asked. Her mind was spinning. It was quite a jump from a spa to bottling mineral water. Did Zeb know what he was talking about? "First I have no way to haul the water in and out of the resort."

"There's where you need to ask your neighbors for help. That nice Bowie boy, for example."

"You mean Sam?" Chloe asked innocently.

"No, I don't mean Sam," he growled. "I mean the sexy, good-looking one."

"I guess I haven't met him yet," she said, wiping her hands with a paper napkin.

He shifted over to her side of the blanket. "It's time you got acquainted," he said, putting one arm around her shoulder. "Ms. Hudson, meet Zebulon Bowie."

"But Mr. Crane, I already know *him*," she protested.

"Not well enough," he muttered in her ear, then angled her face toward him for a hot, possessive kiss.

She took a quick breath. He'd caught her off guard. She didn't expect…this. Yet she'd wanted it. Longed for it. With his hungry mouth on hers, her body came to life. Shockingly, vibrantly to life. She ran one hand through his wheat-colored hair, loving the feel of the thick strands against her sensitive fingers.

Loving the earthy smell of him, the sight of his body, all muscle and sinew, packaged in scuffed boots and wrinkled jeans. Oh my, it was happening again. Her heart was beating wildly. If it hadn't been for the rock behind her, she'd be on her back now with him on top of her. The sun was beating down, turning her into a puddle of pure sexual desire. If she didn't break away now they'd end up on his blanket under a dazzling Colorado sky.

With all the self-control she could muster, and with both hands on his shoulders, she pushed him away, jumped to her feet, ran to the nearest pine tree and leaned against it, breathing hard. In a split second, he was there too, bracing his hands against the tree trunk, effectively trapping her. His eyes glittered dangerously. His lips curved in a ruthless, predatory grin. She shivered in the hot summer sunshine.

"Do you want the money or not?" he demanded.

"Yes, yes," she breathed.

"Then submit to the will of Zebulon Bowie."

"That cad? Never."

"Don't ever say never," he warned, leaning her back into the tree and seizing her mouth in one single take-no-prisoners lunge, plundering deeply, dragging her with him on another wild ride. This time under the sun and not the stars. This time there was nowhere to hide. This time everything was out in the open. There was no escape. No place to go. Not that she wanted to go anywhere. She was already where she wanted to be.

Frantic with need, and tired of games, she knotted her hands around his neck and gave in to her deepest desire. Yes, yes, yes. The words whirled around in her brain. Yes, she wanted the money. But more than that, she wanted him. She wanted him to make love to her. One more time. One last time and then they'd fold up the blanket and go back to the real world.

She should have known there was no world more real than the one they created and no one more real than Zeb Bowie. He was sun and earth and fire and water. He undressed her there under the tree with a gentleness she'd never felt, never known. His fingers moved slowly, deliberately, burning through her clothes wherever, whenever they touched. He worked so slowly her whole body was aching for release by the time he'd unhooked her lace bra and tugged at her bikini underwear.

Standing there in the warm summer sunlight, she should have been too embarrassed to let him stare at her like that, seemingly awestruck, and hear him mutter how lovely she was, and how much he wanted her. Somehow at that moment in time, in that remote rock garden, on top of that mountain, his words and his gaze poured over her like liquid sunshine, making her feel loved and lovely and whole once again.

He kissed her shoulders, he trailed tender kisses down her throat. The peaks of her breasts were taut, so ripe and ready she thought she'd die if he didn't take them into his mouth. When he finally did, gently sucking until she thought she might die of sheer ecstasy, her knees buckled. He caught her around the waist before she sank to the ground.

"Zeb," she whispered, reaching frantically for his

shirt. Pulling it loose, letting her palms slide up his chest and tangle in the crisp hair there. "Oh, Zeb," she sighed. "I know it's wrong, but I want you so much."

"How could anything that feels this right be wrong?" he asked.

Her answer was to frame his face with her hands, to look into his eyes for reassurance. What she saw was the sky reflected there, and beyond that his soul bared for her to see.

"Do you still think you're using me?" he asked.

"No, yes, maybe. I don't know. If you don't care then I don't care. Are you...are you ever going to take your clothes off?" she asked softly.

"Oh, babe," he said ripping off his jeans to free his throbbing erection. "See what you do to me?" He groaned and sank down to his knees to worship at her pedestal. With rapt fervor, he trailed kisses up her thighs and he parted the petals at the juncture of her thighs with his tongue and stroked her intimately until she whispered a plea and begged for release.

"I can't...I can't stand," she said, sinking to her knees next to him until they were chest to chest, thigh to thigh. He tilted her head back and plunged his tongue into her mouth, tangling, dueling. The sounds she made in the back of her throat only urged him on. Until his knees, riddled with sharp needles, couldn't take any more. He stood, pulled her up with him, and flung her over his shoulder, one broad hand cupping her firm bare bottom, to the picnic blanket in the full sunshine where he laid her out flat so he could admire her—with his words, with his clever fingers and with his mouth.

"Have I told you how beautiful you are?" he asked in a hushed voice.

She hoped it was a rhetorical question, because she was beyond answering. All she could do was arch her body to give him better access. She wanted to feel him climax inside her, she wanted him to make her whole again. But he wasn't ready. He *looked* ready, but obviously he wasn't. He wanted to drive her crazy first. Crazy with desire and need.

He worked his way up her body with his mouth, starting with her toes, making them tingle. Making her realize that she had erogenous zones she'd never dreamed of. Her toes, her knees, her inner thighs. And then he was back to those soft, slick petals he'd stroked before. She was only seconds from a climax, milliseconds now before she exploded into a thousand pieces of light. "Yes," she called into the clear mountain air. "Oh, yes." She sobbed uncontrollably and his arms went around her and he held her as the tears trickled down her face and onto his suntanned shoulders.

When the tears stopped falling, she reached to take his arousal in her hand and stroke it, loving the velvet softness of the shaft, loving the power she had to make him come alive. Muttering something desperate, he grasped her hips and let her guide him inside her where he fit as if he belonged there. With deep rhythmic thrusts he brought her to the brink again. Together they rocked into a spiral of ecstasy, higher and higher until they were swept together over the brink into oblivion.

As she lay there, her head pillowed on his shoulder, his arm around her, with the warm sun caressing

their bodies, she wished for only one thing. That she
had the power to make him love her. Because, God
help her, she was afraid…terribly afraid…she was
falling in love with him.

Eight

When Zeb got home after an afternoon of lovemaking beyond his wildest, most incredible dreams, his head was still spinning, his hands still shaking. His senses were still full of her, the scent of her hair, the silken touch of her skin. He was drained, and at the same time filled to the brim, complete for the first time since...for the first time in his life.

He drove down the potholed road with a helpless smile on his lips and an incredible sense that all was right with the world. Which of course, it wasn't. He realized that as he parked in front of the ranch house and it all came back to him. The money, the land, the dam. He'd forgotten everything while in that rock garden. Everything but her. Pleasing her, teasing her, loving her. She made him feel like he could do anything. Be anything. Back at the ranch, he knew he couldn't. Not without her help. He found Sam in the barn feeding the horses. His brother set the bucket of oats on the ground and held out his hands palms up. "Well?"

"There's good news and there's bad news."

"Gimme the bad first."

"We didn't get the loan."

Sam's shoulders sagged.

"The good news is, neither did she."

"She? Who? Never mind, when you say *she* with that look on your face I know who you mean."

"What look?" Sam asked, stuffing his hands in his back pockets.

"You know what look. Like the cat that got the cream."

Zeb felt the heat creep up the back of his neck. He turned to stroke the head of his favorite filly. "Can we talk about the money?"

"Sure that's what's really on your mind?"

"It's always on my mind. Night and day." He didn't say that there was something else, *someone* else, on his mind night and day. But Sam had a way of knowing these things. "No loan, no land. I ran into Ms. Hudson at the bank and talked her out of asking Archie for a loan to develop her property. If I hadn't, he would have told her about the dam, and my name would be mud or worse."

"It's just a matter of time before she finds out," Sam said. "Maybe she ought to find out from us before she hears it from someone else."

"Oh, sure, and then what? We give up, sell the land, rent a space from the fairground and live in our horse trailer? I had a better idea. At least she thought was all right when I suggested it as an alternative to jumping into the spa business without sufficient capital. I told her she ought to start a small business bottling her springwater and selling it.''

"Good idea. But how's it going to help us?" Sam asked.

"You oaf. She'll never be able to bottle and sell her water. Not by herself.''

"Then we'll help her," Sam suggested. "We've got the truck, access to the springs, and we know the territory.''

Zeb's stared at his brother in openmouthed surprise. "Sometimes I wonder about you. Let's reiterate our objectives. We need money. Right? We can't get it from the bank. That leaves Paradise Springs. What stands in our way? Chloe. We have to get rid of Chloe, right?" If that was right, then why did the words stick in his throat? Why did the idea of her leaving Paradise Springs make him feel like he'd been kicked in the groin?

Sam nodded, propping one foot on a bale of hay.

"We have a way of getting rid of her. By letting her see how impractical her plans are. She'll get discouraged when she sees how hard it is to bottle water and sell it. It won't take a rocket scientist to figure out it's even harder to build a spa on that property.''

"We could hammer away at her," Sam said, "but we've already tried that. She's tougher than we thought.''

"Right," Zeb admitted reluctantly. Tougher, yes. But tender, oh so tender and so achingly lovely. And so vulnerable. He couldn't, no he couldn't hammer away, not anymore. Because everything was different now. Since this afternoon everything had changed.

"Let me get this straight," Sam said. "You told her to start a small business, knowing she couldn't possibly do it on her own."

"There's a remote possibility. She's very resourceful, and she's got a settlement from her divorce. And—" he paused and took a deep breath "—she's got us. I suggested that we'd help her."

"Huh?" Sam faced his brother with his hands on his hips. "I'm so confused. Do you want to help this lady or not? I don't know whether you want her to go or to stay. I've seen the way you look at her. Like she's a hot biscuit just out of the oven, slathered with butter and honey…"

Zeb swallowed hard, remembering how sweet her lips were, with or without the honey. "Funny you should mention that."

"And I've seen the way she looks at you…"

"I don't want to hear this," he said. But he knew the way she looked at him, with those meltingly soft brown eyes, like he was some kind of superhero who knew everything. That was not the issue. If it was, he would have followed her home, followed her anywhere just to bask in the light of those eyes. "We've got some hard decisions to make here," he reminded himself as well as his brother.

"Sounds like you've already made them. We help her. We discourage her. We tell her to go home because we want her land. But we want her to stay, because…because…?" Sam stood there along with the horses in their stalls, their heads turned in his direction, all of them staring at Zeb, waiting for an answer.

"We *don't* want her to stay. It would be a terrible mistake for her to stay," Zeb said firmly. "She doesn't belong here. Even you can see that. She's a city girl. She's been married once. To a doctor. She'll get married again. A woman like that, she's got everything. She's a great cook, she's great in...in every way. Except for an excess of stubbornness, but that could be overcome, with the right man."

"You wouldn't be the right man, would you?" Sam asked, not bothering to conceal his knowing grin.

"For Chloe Hudson?" Zeb asked incredulously. "Are you crazy? I'm not right for her and she's not right for me. Nobody's right for me except for a good time now and then. I think you know that. I'm not marriage material."

"Who said that?"

"Joanne said that."

"Forget that. She didn't know what she was talking about," Sam said.

Zeb couldn't forget it. Couldn't forget how he felt when he found out she'd left. So stupid, so naive, so duped. He vowed then no woman would ever make him feel that way again. And they hadn't.

"Talking about this makes me hungry," Sam said. "George left a pot of chili on the stove. Think we should invite Chloe?"

"No," Zeb burst out.

"But we owe her," Sam protested. "After all she did for us last night."

"I bought her lunch today," Zeb explained.

"That was nice of you," Sam said turning toward the door.

"Yeah, but I can't do that every day." But oh, how he'd like to. How he'd like to make love to her every long, lazy afternoon. "It takes too much time, too much...besides, it's not fair, not fair to her."

Sam gave him a puzzled look. "But tomorrow we're going over there to help her bottle her water," he said. "Aren't we?"

"That's what I said, didn't I? We're going to help her get ready to bottle her water and then we're going to butt out and let her fail. Is that clear?" he demanded. What was wrong with his little brother that he couldn't understand this elementary concept? That he wanted her to go, but he wanted her to stay. That he didn't want to help her, because the more he helped her the more he wanted to help her and that was just no good.

Sam shrugged, but Zeb had the feeling he understood much more than Zeb wanted him to.

Chloe didn't know much about bottling springwater, but she did know she ought to collect samples. So before it got dark, she went around putting water in old gin bottles that were stashed in one of the cabins. All the while, she pictured the bottles on the shelf of the grocery store. Not the old gin bottles, but clean bottles filled with sparkling water and labeled Paradise Springs. Picturing the sales figures, the advertisements, the booming business.

And all of it thanks to Zeb Bowie. As she heated a can of soup over an open fire that evening, she remembered her first impression of him. A randy,

flirtatious cowboy, interested in nothing but a hot
soak and a hot roll in the hay. But he was so much
more. An enterprising businessman. A tender and
considerate lover.

Considerate? Yes, he was that and so much more.
Inspired. Imaginative. Intense. Divine. She could go
on all night. And she probably would. Go on thinking
about what had happened that afternoon. Remembering the last kiss at the side of the road, when he
let her out of his truck, a kiss that rocked her to the
tips of her toes. A kiss that promised more to come.

She'd stood there in the road watching his truck
weave its way to his ranch, wondering if he too had
felt the earth move when they kissed. If his life had
been turned upside down the way hers had been in
one magical, wondrous summer afternoon. Who was
it that said that ''summer afternoon'' were the two
most beautiful words in the English language? Whoever it was must have spent a summer afternoon in
the garden of the gods, surrounded by red rocks and
fragrant pines, making love to Zeb Bowie.

She didn't know where it was all leading. At the
moment she didn't care. She only knew she was a
different person from the woman who'd staggered up
that trail with her suitcase and her portable coffeemaker. She no longer staggered. She was more physically fit than she'd ever been, and was on her way
to becoming emotionally fit, too. Thanks to Zeb, she
felt lovable again. Maybe he didn't love her, he
didn't say he did, but he made her *feel* that way. She
fell asleep with a smile on her face and hope in her
heart. The fervent hope that she could make a go of

her new business and even more outrageous hope
that Zeb would fall in love with her.

The next day Zeb and Sam appeared at the springs
early, ready to help her out. Her hopes surged. Her
heart filled with gratitude. But she didn't speak a
word. She didn't know what to say. Whether to mention yesterday, or talk about the weather. She didn't
have to. Between the Bowie brothers, they kept up a
steady patter, half kidding, half arguing. Chloe was
grateful for the noise, because her vocal chords
weren't working. Zeb didn't appear to notice.

She noticed Zeb though. Especially when he
stripped down to his low-slung jeans and worked half
naked under the hot sun to clear a space on his road
so delivery trucks would have access to her property.
He convinced her she'd need room for the trucks that
would pick up the bottles of her delicious springwater and deliver it to the markets. As he worked,
his muscles rippled and the sweat poured off his sun-
bronzed shoulders. He sawed trees, she dragged
branches. He hacked at roots, she watched when he
wasn't looking.

Her fingers itched to touch him, to press her palms
against his chest, to feel his heartbeat, to slide her
hands down under his tight jeans. Oh Lord, she was
losing her composure, her self-control. Now she
wondered if he'd say anything about yesterday. She
tore her eyes away from his beautiful body and threw
herself into the hard work. Perspiration dripped off
her forehead. Her shirt stuck to her back.

Finally, after a long morning's work, she limped
back to her site to throw together some kind of lunch.

Her back hurt, her legs were sore. But she owed them lunch. She owed them a lot more than that. But she had the feeling they wouldn't take money. The Bowie brothers were strong, they were willing and they were the hardest workers she'd ever seen. Thank God for the work. Without it she might have blurted out something stupid. She might have asked for some kind of reassurance that he hadn't forgotten about yesterday, that it had meant something to him.

She made a huge cheese-and-wild-onion omelet and hashed brown potatoes for the three of them. They sat on the ground, drank springwater and ate ravenously after their hard physical labour.

"You're right, Zeb," Sam said between bites. "She is a good cook."

Zeb nodded and Chloe smiled modestly.

"Hear he took you to lunch yesterday," Sam said.

"We had a picnic," Chloe said, finding her voice at last.

"A picnic? No kidding? With ants and bees and grass and all that?" Sam asked with a sideways glance at his brother.

"I…didn't notice any ants," Chloe said, her eyes on her tin plate.

"What did you notice?" Zeb asked with a pointed look in her direction.

Chloe took a long drink of cold water to try to cool the heat that flooded her face. And decided to ignore the question. "Of course every day's a picnic since I got here," she said.

"If you like it now, you should see it in the winter," Sam said. "It's beautiful."

"If you like ice and snow," Zeb interjected.

"I don't know. I've never seen it," she said.

"Never seen snow?" Sam asked. "How old are you?"

"Thirty-two."

"Thirty-two and she's never seen snow. Did you hear that, Zeb?"

"I heard it," Zeb said. She felt his eyes on her, watching her, assessing her. Did he think she couldn't take a winter here? Maybe she couldn't.

"I guess my mineral-water business will only be open in the summers. Same for my spa."

"What will you do in the winter?" Sam asked.

"Go back to my job. I'm a nurse."

"She's a nurse. Did you hear that, Zeb?"

"Of course I heard it. I'm not deaf. I hear everything she says," Zeb said, throwing a handful of pebbles at his brother.

Sam responded by tossing a cup of water in his brother's face.

Chloe ducked and moved out of the line of fire.

"You're making Chloe glad she's an only child," Zeb warned.

"Is she?"

"Are you?"

"No, I have an older sister. But we never fight like this. It's disgraceful to see grown men assault each other physically. Especially blood brothers. My sister has never thrown a stone at me and I've never thrown water in her face. It wouldn't be dignified," she said primly.

"Disgraceful," Zeb muttered. "Wouldn't be dignified." Then with a wicked grin he threw a cup of water in Chloe's face, drenching her hair and her shirt as well as her face.

It was icy cold. She sat there, stunned. Then her mouth flew open and she sputtered. "How dare you...how dare you—" She picked up her cup and flung her water at Zeb.

He laughed and grabbed her around the waist. Her cup slipped from her fingers and bounced on the hard ground.

"Think I'll go home now. See ya tomorrow, Chloe," Sam said with a wink at his brother over his shoulder as he walked down the trail toward the ranch.

As Sam's footsteps faded away, it was suddenly quiet. Except for a flock of quail who scattered as Sam passed. Zeb's laughter died in his throat as his gaze held hers for a long moment.

His arms tightened around her, and she panicked. This could get to be a habit, this love in the afternoon. Zeb could get to be a habit, a habit she would have one awful time breaking. She wanted him now, she'd wanted him all night. But he wanted a summer romance. She didn't. The next time she gave her heart away it would be forever. Not that she was ever going to get married again, but if she did...

"I...I really should get back to work," she said, her lips only an inch from his. If she leaned forward just an inch she could close the gap between them. For one long moment they stood there, waiting for the other to make the first move. On the outside she was shaking from the cold water that clung to her hair and her shirt. But inside she was burning like a hot furnace.

After an eternity of waiting, he made his move. His hands were in her wet hair as he crushed her to him, bringing her mouth to his over and over for deep, soulful kisses. Letting his tongue slide into her mouth and merge with hers.

When he came up for air he said, "Me, too, gotta get back to work. My boss is a slave driver." He kissed her again, long, and lingering. "You taste…so good…. Boss."

His chest was bare.

Her shirt was damp. She wanted to take it off. She wanted him to take it off. To feel the hair on his chest brush against her sensitive nipples. Just thinking about it made them bead and quiver. No. She couldn't, wouldn't, shouldn't.

"This could get to be a habit," she murmured, her hands on his bare shoulders.

"Sounds good to me," he said with that sexy grin he did so well.

"Yes, but I don't want a summer romance."

"What do you want? Winter, spring, fall? I can arrange that." He traced one callused finger around her cheek and then brushed her lower lip with his thumb, with such tenderness she felt tears welling. Here she was, in danger of spending another afternoon making wild passionate love with a man she should definitely not fall in love with. Not if she valued her hard-won independence.

She took his hand away and took a deep breath. "What do I want? I want to be self-sufficient. I don't want to depend on anyone and I don't want anyone to depend on me. I don't want anyone to have the power to walk out on me or tell me lies. I don't want to fall in love again. I'm not going to fall in love again. Do you understand that?''

He nodded, his arms at his sides. ''Sweetheart, nobody understands better than me. But that has nothing to do with us. We've both been burned. We're not going to take any more chances. We're perfect for each other.''

Perfect for him, yes. Perfect for her, no. He'd take and she'd give. And at the end of the summer she'd leave. He'd have no regrets, just memories. Maybe. And she'd be in the same fix she was when Brandon left her. No, worse.

''No thanks,'' she said.

''What?''

''I can't do this, this short-term stuff. I can't do long-term either. So that pretty much lets me out of the game,'' she said with a small smile.

He shrugged and reached for his shirt, which he'd hung on a branch. Then he stuck out his hand. ''Still friends?''

She smiled and shook his hand. ''Friends.''

She watched him go as he whistled his way back down the trail, envying his carefree insouciance. His motto—Take Her or Leave Her. It was all the same to him. Thank God she'd put a stop to it. Otherwise, right now, they might be swinging in her hammock together, her wet shirt hanging next to his on that branch. Her lace bra draped over a wild rosebush, drying in the warm summer breeze, while she... while they... She wrapped her arms around her waist and stifled more than a trace of regret.

The next day they were back again, as if nothing had happened, as if they were her hired help, concentrating on clearing sites for the collection, purification and bottling of her springwater.

"How come you're doing this?" she asked, offering them each a cup of herb tea before they went back to their ranch that afternoon.

"You're our neighbor. We want to help you," Sam said.

"Don't you have work to do at your own place?"

"Yep. But we owe it to you. You know, old Horatio, he helped us plenty of times, plowed our road for us one winter when we'd been snowbound for seven days. Won't ever forget that," Sam said.

"What do you do in the winter?" she asked.

"Repair equipment. Take care of the livestock," Sam said.

"What do *you* do in the winter?" Zeb asked.

"When I'm not on duty, I hang out at my neighborhood coffeehouse, drink lattes and watch the rain." It sounded so urbane, so effete. She wondered for a moment if she could go back to her old life. What was wrong with her? Of course she could.

"She misses her coffee," Zeb explained to Sam. "Wouldn't touch mine."

"Someday, when I have my spa and electric power, I'll have espressos and lattes and... What about my water business? Will I need electricity?"

Zeb shook his head and took a notebook out of his pocket and made a note. "Gas-driven pump should work."

"Pump? I thought I'd fill the bottles straight from the stream. Then drive them into town. Keep it simple, at least at first."

Zeb and Sam exchanged a look that contained pity for her naiveté.

"Okay, what do I need besides a gas-driven pump?"

"Water tank to hold the water you pump out of your stream. Plastic pipe to carry the water from the stream to the tank. Plastic bottles."

"Oh, but I thought I'd have glass with my Paradise Springs logo on them."

"Too expensive and easy to break. You want plastic gallon jugs. And a filter."

"Why do I need a filter? Isn't the water pure?"

"It may be pure, but there's bound to be sediment in it," Sam said. "Nobody will buy your water if there's a bunch of crud at the bottom of the jug."

"Or little things swimming in it," Zeb said.

"Little things? What kind of little things... Fish?"

"Amoebas, stuff like that."

"I should have it tested first," she said.

"Good thinking," Zeb said, reaching over to take the bottle out of her hands. "We'll take it in for you and have it tested at the county. Wouldn't want to buy a whole lot of equipment if the water's no good."

"Oh, but it's got to be good. Great-Grandpa drank it and hundreds of visitors to Paradise Springs drank it and I drink it." She lifted her tin cup and took a large gulp just to prove it to them. "If you'll tell me where it is, I'll take the water in myself. You've already done more than enough for me. I can't ask you to do any more."

"Sure you can," Zeb said. "We're going that way anyway, so it's no trouble."

"Then I'll go with you."

Zeb and Sam exchanged glances. Her heart fell. They didn't want her along. They were going somewhere else along the way. Somewhere that she couldn't come.

"Never mind, I'll go by myself," she said.

"No. We'll all go together," Zeb said.

"Are you sure?" she asked. She didn't want them to think she didn't appreciate what they were doing for her. But she didn't want to be left out of the loop. It was her land, and her mineral springs and she was going to be a part of this business every step of the way.

After considerable discussion between the brothers, which seemed to go on for another half hour, it turned out Thursday was the best day for a trip to the county building in nearby McClure. They were back before that though, the next afternoon, tramping up and down, following the stream, trying to pick a spot for the tank, another for the pump.

"The tank should be downstream to take advantage of gravity," Sam said, resting his shovel on his shoulder.

"Uh-huh. The obvious place for the tank is up there. As long as she's got a pump she doesn't need to rely on gravity, so that's the way to go." Zeb pointed to a flat clearing on the top of a slope. "It's a perfect place to fill the bottles and load them into her truck."

"She doesn't have a truck," Sam protested.

"I could..." she said.

"She can borrow ours to start with, but eventually she'll have to get one," Zeb said.

"I couldn't…" she said.

Zeb interrupted. "Eventually she'll need a conveyor belt and an assembly line, someone to fill, someone to cap, someone to…"

"Wait a second," she said. "Can I say something? I don't want a big operation here. Or a big staff to supervise. You know, that's what happened to me in nursing. I was booted up to administration and then I didn't get to do any patient care any more. Here I have a chance to start small and stay small. Isn't that what you said the banker wanted?"

"Right," Zeb said. "Sorry. I got carried away. I can't help myself. Your project is exciting. Has potential."

"I'm surprised my great-grandfather didn't think of it."

"Yeah, well…he had his hands full just holding things together." He stood his shovel against a tree. "We'll see you Thursday," he said. Then they took off down the trail.

Chloe watched them go, knowing she was the one who'd put an end to her relationship with Zeb, if that's what you could call it. It was *her* idea to be friends with him. She just hadn't expected him to agree so fast. To come every day and do some work and then leave. She was grateful for his help, even more grateful for his restraint, because heaven knew she didn't have any. So why was she standing there, feeling let down and left out? Missing his searing kisses, his strong arms around her, his eyes burning hot with desire. Wishing he'd at least kissed her goodbye. Or said something—anything—to make her think he cared.

* * *

On Thursday Zeb and Sam picked Chloe up, and soon she was wedged between the two brothers in the front seat of their truck, while her box of samples rattled against each other in the back. Zeb soon realized that putting Chloe between himself and Sam was not a good idea. Because at every curve in the road, she was pitched against him, her thigh meshed with his, her shoulder pressed against his, causing an instant reaction of hot, undeniable desire.

He'd been so proud of his abstinence, of his ability to walk away from her every day. Taking her at her word that she only wanted to be friends had been difficult, though not impossible. But not today. Today it seemed difficult *and* impossible. All he could think about was getting her alone, finding a meadow, a hill, in the sun or under the moon, and making mad, passionate love to her all over again.

But it wasn't going to happen. It wasn't fair to her and it wasn't fair to him. Neither one of them needed another rejection in their lives. Another breakup. Both of which were inevitable.

"I appreciate you guys not pressuring me to sell you the springs anymore," she said, tightening her seat belt.

"That's not our way," Zeb said. "After all, you can catch more flies with honey than with vinegar."

He noticed that she gave him a puzzled look out of the corner of her eye. Probably wondering what he was talking about. Why did he have to mention honey? It just made him remember that morning when she'd licked the honey off his lips. He shifted in the driver's seat, trying to get his mind off that incident at his ranch and back to the task at hand.

"I'm glad you finally realize that selling out is the last thing I'd ever do," she continued. "Even if nothing comes of the springwater idea, I'll still have my spa. Some day. Somehow."

Somewhere, he added fervently but silently. Somewhere else, anywhere but Paradise Springs.

"Did you ever buy that bull you were looking for?" she asked.

"Not yet," Zeb said through clenched teeth, knowing only too well that it was her stubborn refusal to sell the land that prevented them from buying the bull.

"We're using studs from other ranches," Sam explained. "It's expensive but not as expensive as buying a bull. See, we had a run of bad luck last year, an anthrax epidemic killed part of our herd along with our bull, and then there was the flood."

Zeb shot Sam a murderous look. The word flood should not be mentioned in Chloe's presence. It might lead to talk of a dam. Fortunately, Sam got the message and didn't say anything else. But Chloe did.

"What flood was that?" she asked. "Did it affect my property?"

"Not really," Zeb said briskly. "But we lost a whole crop. Had to buy feed for our cattle."

"Set us back a few grand," Sam added.

"I know you went to the bank for money," she said, staring at the long road ahead, "and I know why you need the money. I also know you got turned down. So I don't see how you're going to get out of the hole. Enough to buy a bull. Let alone make me an offer on my property. Two things I don't understand. Why you want it and how you were going to pay for it.''

"I thought you didn't want to talk about selling us your property. If you do..." Zeb said.

"No...no, I'd rather not. I just wondered, that's all.''

Zeb heaved a silent sigh of relief and changed the subject to discuss the virtues of shorthorn cattle versus Hereford with his brother. They went on to the type of feed that was best for each. Chloe yawned, leaned back against the vinyl seat and closed her eyes. Her head drifted toward Zeb's shoulder and settled there so comfortably that he instantly lost his train of thought.

Her hair brushed his collar, her scent threatened to overwhelm him. He gripped the steering wheel tightly so he wouldn't be tempted to put his arm around her. For one thing, Sam would be shocked and for another, they were just friends. Just friends—yeah, right.

Sam brought up the subject of what was more important in a stud, looks or family history. As usual, they debated this loudly.

"Short legs, a stumpy neck and a bulky body is worth all the pedigrees in the world," Sam said.

"That's where you're wrong. Looks come and go. But breeding, breeding will always tell. Cream rises to the top," Zeb said.

"What about character?" Chloe said, blinking and sitting up straight.

Sam and Zeb stopped talking and looked at her.

"What does that mean?" Zeb asked warily.

"Character? Honesty, integrity and principle."

"How do you judge character?" Zeb asked with a puzzled frown.

"I used to think you could use your instincts," she said, staring out the window at the distant mountains. "But that doesn't always work. So now I don't know. Personally, I've lost my confidence in instinct. That's why I'm never getting married again."

"What are you talking about?" Zeb asked her.

"What are *you* talking about?" she returned, looking from one to the other.

"Bulls. They don't have any character, not so's you'd notice. They're all the same. They're bullies," Sam said.

"Oh. I thought…never mind," Chloe said, closing her eyes and resting her head lightly on the rear truck window.

"Character…" Zeb muttered. "Yeah, we'll have to look for a bull with character."

After another half hour during which Chloe either slept or pretended to sleep so she wouldn't make a fool of herself again, they arrived in McClure, the county seat, with its town square, courthouse and fairgrounds. While Sam went to look up a friend, Chloe and Zeb left the water samples off at a small lab in the basement of the county building where they learned it would take a few weeks to get the results.

Chloe's face fell. "I can't wait a few weeks," she told Zeb. "I have to get the results so I can get the loan so I can make plans, buy equipment and winterize one of the cabins so I can store my stuff there." She shook her head, suddenly overwhelmed with the enormity of the project. "I don't know. Maybe this isn't such a good idea, after all."

Zeb stared at her, opened his mouth to speak, then changed his mind and closed it.

"Everything's so different from what I imagined." She rubbed her forehead. "I was so naive, I thought I could get a loan and open a spa just like that. I can't even start a mineral-water business without…" She looked around at the tan institutional walls. "Without a lot of bureaucratic red tape and a lot of work and… Oh, Zeb, what am I doing?" she asked.

"Doing? You're starting a business. You can't give up now." He took her by the shoulders and held her tight, looking deep into her eyes. She gave him a tentative smile and his heart surged. Did his encouragement mean so much to her? She was so vulnerable. Sometimes so sure of herself and other times so insecure. But what was he doing? What was he saying? He *wanted* her to give up.

"Do you really think I can do it?" she asked, lifting her face to his, her trusting gaze fastened on his.

"Of course you can. If you want to bad enough. But why don't you slow down and relax and enjoy the springs while you can?"

"While I can? What does that mean?"

"It means…that once you get the word on the water and actually start bottling, you won't have any spare time." Whew. Back on track. He'd felt himself waffling for a minute. Hating to see her discouraged. Wanting to see her succeed. Forgetting that her success was his failure. But he got out of it. What he'd really meant was that Paradise Springs would not be there forever and she ought to enjoy it while she could.

"If you really believe in me," she said, her eyes brimming over with hope and confidence, "then maybe I'd better extend my leave at the hospital. And if they say no, I've got better things to do."

Zeb's heart sank. Extend her leave. Better things to do. "Don't do anything rash," he warned. "You don't want to jeopardize your job or anything."

"Why not? The more I think about going back there and doing the same old thing every day, the less it appeals to me. Whereas here, every day is a new challenge."

"You can say that again," Zeb muttered. "And if you like challenges, you'll love winter," he reminded her grimly.

As he walked briskly down the corridor and out the door, he shook his head, afraid she hadn't heard him, afraid she wasn't going to give up after all. And it was his fault. No, it was her fault. She made him do things he shouldn't do, say things he shouldn't say. Not if he wanted to hold on to the ranch for the next generation of Bowies. Maybe there wouldn't be any more Bowies. Sam showed no inclination to get married. And if it was up to him, the line would die out. Because he was *never* getting married.

Nine

Chloe found a pay phone in the hallway of the county building and while Zeb went to price fencing at the farm-supply store, she called her friend and supervisor at the hospital in San Francisco.

"Chloe! Where on earth are you?" Cass asked.

"In Colorado at my property. Actually I'm thirty miles away at the county seat in McClure. I came to have my water tested," Chloe said.

"What?"

"I'm planning to bottle and sell my mineral water."

"What about the spa? My vacation's coming up and I'm ready for a week of pampering and massages," Cass said.

"Don't pack your bags yet. The place needs a little work. I'm going to do it, though. I'm definitely going to do it. It just might take a little longer than I thought. It's...it's kind of remote.''

"Remote? That's okay. I want to get away from it all.''

"Do you want to take a three-mile hike just to get there?''

"Three miles?'' Cass said, alarmed.

"Uphill.'' Might as well tell it like it was.

"That *is* remote.'' Cass's voice fell.

Remote was only the half of it. It was not only remote, it was downright ramshackle. "And at the moment there's no electricity or phones.''

"Okay, I get the picture. Maybe I'll go to Costa del Oro and have the shiatsu massage. Why don't you come with me? Aren't you lonely there?''

"Not really. I have neighbors. The Bowie brothers. Cattle ranchers.''

"Ooh, do they wear Stetsons and leather boots and lasso cows all day?'' Cass asked.

"They're more into breeding.'' Chloe's face reddened, remembering how she'd blundered into the middle of their conversation today. "They're very helpful.''

"In what way?'' Cass asked.

Chloe listed all the things they did for her, wondering what on earth she would have done without them, her pulse rate increasing as she pictured Zeb digging a post hole for her with his shirt off, his hair in his face, his rugged torso drenched with sweat.

"I was just wondering...'' Chloe took a deep breath. "Because things are moving so slowly here...what would you think if I didn't come back in the fall, if I took the whole year off?''

"No, you can't. I need you. I have no one to talk to. And Brandon broke up with that nurse in the ER."

"Really."

"Really. She transferred to ICU. He was asking about you. Said he was hurt you hadn't told him you were leaving. I think he misses you."

"Well, I don't miss him. It's so different here. People are more real, close to the earth, honest, trustworthy."

"People? Or one of those cowboys next door?"

Cass always was perceptive. She knew about Brandon way before Chloe did. But then so did everyone.

"You're not falling for one of those cowboys, are you, Chloe?" Cass asked. "Of course if they're anything like they are in the movies."

Chloe gripped the receiver remembering the first time she'd seen Zeb stepping out of the tub, clasping his hat in his hand, covering his...

"Nothing like that," Chloe said. It was true. Zeb was not a movie star. He was a real man. Down-to-earth, tough, tender, funny, sweet, warm, caring...

"Remember you've been hurt. You're in a vulnerable state," Cass warned.

"Not anymore. I've got my confidence back. I can do anything. Bottle mineral water, build a spa out of a broken-down hot-springs resort, and..." She almost said, *fall in love again,* but she didn't. She *had* fallen in love again. But she knew what Cass would say. *It's too soon. You're on the rebound.* She might ask, *Does he love you?* And she'd have to admit that he didn't. And even if he did, he wasn't going to get married. But maybe if she stuck around and he got used to having her around, and learned to trust her, to believe she wouldn't walk out on him...

"And what?" Cass asked.

"Nothing. Well, I've got to go."

"Don't do anything rash. We want you back. We expect you back. We *need* you back."

Chloe hung up, feeling torn in two directions. Despite her newfound confidence, she wasn't at all sure she could make a success of bottling water, building a spa or making Zeb Bowie fall in love with her. Whereas she was wanted, needed and expected back at her job.

As she walked down the street to where the truck was parked, she glanced up at the cumulus clouds that billowed above the county courthouse. *What do you think, Great-Grandpa?* she asked. *Do I have a chance, a chance to rejuvenate Paradise Hot Springs, to make Zeb fall in love with me?* A sudden gust of wind blew an old newspaper in her path. She glanced down at the headline. Flooding Persists. New Hope for Proponents of Dam Site.

So much for her hopes of a message from Great-Grandpa Horatio to come blowing her way. Something on the order of "Go For It," or "Get out while the getting's good." Thinking the Bowies might be interested in the article about flooding, she picked it up and stuffed it in her purse.

Zeb threw a roll of fencing into the back of the truck while Sam watched.

"Where is she?" Sam asked, looking at his watch. "We gotta be getting back."

"Making a phone call. We're not in such a hurry. We have time for coffee at that new coffeehouse. Chloe loves good coffee, and I thought we'd all have a latte."

"You thought we'd all have a *latte*? How do you even know what a latte is? What is it with you and Chloe, anyway?"

"Nothing."

"Yeah, right. You think I'm blind? Think I can't see you're falling in love with her?"

"What?" Zeb asked indignantly.

"What's gonna happen when she finds out you're not a man of character. That you've got no honesty, integrity or principles."

"She won't find out. Or when she does, she'll be a thousand miles away. Back where she belongs. She's calling her hospital right now. They'll talk her into coming back. They'd be crazy to let her go. If you had Chloe, would you let her go?" Zeb demanded.

Sam leaned against the tailgate and stared at him. "But I don't. And neither do you. You don't have her and you don't want her. That's what you said, isn't it?"

Zeb slumped against the door of the truck and stared down the street without even seeing the catalog outlet and the yogurt shop. He didn't have Chloe and he never would. "I do want her," he admitted for the first time. "But I've already been that route. I had my chance to get married and I blew it."

"What are you talking about? You didn't blow it, Joanne did."

Zeb shook his head. "That's not what everyone in town said."

"You're wrong. Everyone in town said that you were lucky to get off so easy. That you were too good for her. You deserved better. You deserve a second chance."

Zeb looked at his little brother standing there, propped against his truck. Once he'd been a little kid who needed rescuing from the bullies in the schoolyard, and now he was a good inch taller than Zeb. Suddenly Sam looked so old and sounded so wise he almost didn't recognize him.

"You think so?" Zeb asked gruffly, a faint stirring of hope in his heart.

"I know so," Sam said firmly. "Here she comes. Come on, let's go get a latte."

"I'm gonna have to tell her," Zeb said grabbing Sam by the arm. "Tell her everything."

"Yeah," Sam said.

But he couldn't tell her anything at the coffeehouse. It was too crowded, too noisy. Not on the way home, either. When he asked her if she'd extended her leave, she was noncommittal. Pensive all the way home. They all were. No one spoke. He'd wait until they were alone. Tomorrow.

But tomorrow came and went. A calf got sick. He had to sit up all night with it. The work didn't bother him. He couldn't sleep anyway. He was trying to think of what to say to her. How to say that he loved her. Even though he'd lied to her from the first moment he'd seen her. Why should she believe him? What if she didn't love him, didn't want to stay? What if she'd already decided to go home? What would she say when she found out they were going to flood the Springs? Why would she stay if she couldn't have her spa? Why should she stay just for him? Joanne hadn't been willing to.

Chloe almost forgot about the clipping. It was two days later by the time she got around to digging it out of her purse. She sat on the edge of her inflatable air mattress and unfolded the old newspaper she'd forgotten to give to Zeb and Sam. It would be of interest to them because, according to the map, the dam would be built upriver from their property. And according to the map, Paradise Springs would be sold to the Bureau of Reclamation for fair market value and flooded.

She jumped off the bed and almost hit her head on the low ceiling. The newspaper fell to the floor. It couldn't be true. It was an old newspaper, from a month ago. If it was true, they'd know about it. They'd have told her about it. *Someone* would have told her about it. Her inheritance, flooded. The cabins, the orchard, the cold springs, the hot springs, gone. Her future. Gone.

She went out into the cool night air and paced back and forth in the clearing in the dusk. In the morning she'd walk over to the ranch and demand an explanation. But in her heart she knew the explanation. They'd known all along and hadn't told her. Zeb had kept it a secret from her. No, that was impossible. He cared about her. She knew he did. He didn't love her, but he wouldn't lie to her, either.

She tried to sleep that night, but couldn't. She dredged up everything he'd ever said to her. Everything having to do with the property. There was never a hint, never a clue. Or was there? Maybe she hadn't wanted to hear, hadn't wanted to understand that he was eager to buy her property so he could resell it to the Bureau of Reclamation and make a tidy sum. Enough to buy a bull. She remembered everything he'd ever done, all the hard work he'd expended for her...and now she knew the reason for it. To soften her up for the sale. Well, she'd softened, all right. So soft she'd melted into his arms, lost her head and her heart as well.

Lying there in the middle of the night she remembered how he'd made love to her, how close she'd felt to him then, as if she'd found her other half, the part that made her whole. She'd thought he felt the same. But it was all an act. The tears came, hot and heavy, and soaked her flannel sheet.

She should have known he had an ulterior motive. Should have known she was not his type. She was beginning to wonder if she was anyone's type. What had he said? "Fool me once, shame on you, fool me twice, shame on me." Well, she'd been fooled twice and she felt the shame. Her whole body ached, her head throbbed with the shame.

In the morning she'd go to town instead of to the Bar Z Ranch. What good would it do to confront Zeb? He'd just lie to her again. She had to get the truth from another source. An unbiased source. Archibald Crane, the banker. It all came back to her now. Zeb hadn't wanted her to meet Archibald. Because he knew the truth. Everyone knew the truth but her. Wilma, the waitress, Barney, Sam, everyone. She felt so naive.

Before hiking out to her car, she looked around at the cabins and the rusted swimming pool, and finally at the bathhouse. Instead of self-pity, she felt proud of what she'd done there in such a short time. If she had longer…but she didn't. Her time in this beautiful spot was limited. Not just by the threat of the dam, but by her betrayal at the hands of her neighbor. She blinked back the tears that sprang to her eyes, lifted her chin and marched out without a backward glance. She knew the truth, but she had to hear the words spoken. Just once would do. Then she'd leave.

Archibald Crane was charming. He treated her with old-fashioned courtesy, telling her what she already knew in deep, sonorous tones. She only had to sign certain papers, waiving all claim to the property, giving it over to the Bureau of Reclamation, and she'd be in fine financial shape. She'd have more money than Horatio ever dreamed of.

"But, you knew him…would my great-grandfather have wanted to sell?" she asked.

He shrugged. "Horatio was a gambler. He won and lost money, property, horses, cattle. I don't think he attached that much value to a piece of land. Made himself at home wherever the four winds blew him. Very adaptable." The banker fingered his pocket watch and observed Chloe with one raised eyebrow. "I suspect you're much like him. You take things as they come."

"I…don't know. I'd like to be. Tell me, Mr. Crane, I suppose everyone in town knew about the dam being built and how much my property was worth, didn't they?"

"I don't know about everybody."

"My neighbors, the Bowies?" she asked, scarcely realizing she was holding her breath.

"I believe Zeb mentioned it to me the last time he was in the office. Yes, he asked me if I'd heard any word on the dam and I assured him the deal was going through."

The day he'd come to the bank. The same day *she'd* come to the bank. He'd discouraged her from sticking around to see Archibald. Instead he'd taken her on a picnic and made love to her. Made her forget all about getting a loan. Not him. He hadn't forgotten anything. He was thinking, always thinking about how to get her land away from her. Even while he was kissing her, holding her, telling her how beautiful she was. She felt the rage build inside her. Starting at the tips of her toes and rising to the top of her head, like a kettle about to boil over.

She could understand lying, cheating and stealing for land. She could forgive someone for falling in love with a piece of property. She'd done it herself. But he didn't do it for the land. He did it for the money he could make by reselling it. Just for the money. That was all. She wrapped her arms around her waist to keep from shaking uncontrollably.

"Are you all right, little lady?" the banker asked with a worried frown.

"Just fine." She forced a smile, thanked him and left his office. There was only one place to go. Only one thing to do.

Ten

Chloe had never walked so fast in her life as she did on the trail to the Bar Z Ranch. But then she'd never been so mad in her life. Dry twigs snapped under her boots, quail scurried for cover. Like a homing pigeon she headed straight for the corral, though she'd never been there. Zeb was sitting on the top rail watching a calf and its mother with such intense scrutiny he didn't hear her approach.

She cleared her throat. He swiveled and almost fell off the fence.

"Chloe," he said, jumping down and reaching for her. "You're here."

She backed out of his reach. "I'm here, but not for long."

"What do you mean?"

"I've decided to leave. I'm going home."

"Home? What? I thought…"

"When I talked to my supervisor the other day she convinced me to come back right away. They need me."

"*They* need you? What about us? You can't just leave like that."

Chloe had to give him credit. He looked genuinely upset. But that was because she hadn't told him about the land yet.

"Can't I? Why not?"

"What about the bottled water, what about your spa? You're giving all that up?" he asked incredulously.

"It wasn't a very practical idea to have a spa. You said yourself that it was too remote, too rugged. I finally realized that you were right."

His broad forehead creased in a frown. "No, wait a minute. This doesn't make sense. The last time I saw you, you never said anything. You were talking about spending the winter here. The spa was your dream. Now you've changed your mind? I don't believe it."

"Believe it. I realized that spending the winter here would be impossible. I can't imagine being snowed in. I'd go crazy." Despite herself she couldn't help imagining being snowed into Zeb's ranch house with him, making love in front of a roaring fire while the snow piled up outside the window. But that was a dream. Another dream that wouldn't come true.

"We wouldn't have to stay here all winter. We could take a vacation, go to San Francisco if you wanted. We don't have that much to do in the winter.''

"What are you talking about?" she asked.

"I'm talking about you and me," he said, his eyes the intense blue of the sky. "I'm talking about you and me getting together, getting, getting…married."

She shook her head sadly. So that's how desperate he was to get her land. What was it he'd said? "You can catch more flies with honey than with vinegar." Well, this was one fly who wasn't fooled by his honey-eyed tongue. "I thought you weren't marriage material."

"That's what I thought. That's what I'd been told. But that was before I met you. Before I fell in love with you," he blurted.

Her chest hurt, her hands shook. It was painful to see him lie right to her face. It was painful for him too, from the look on his face.

"You're getting carried away," she said stiffly. It was better than saying what she wanted to say. *You're lying.*

"Don't I mean anything to you?" he asked, grabbing her by the shoulders and staring into her eyes.

"Of course. You were my summer romance. And I was yours. Let's leave it at that, can't we?"

"No, we can't," he said tightening his grip on her shoulders. "I can't. I want you around in the fall and spring and winter, too. All the time. If you don't like it here, we'll move to town, let Sam run the ranch. But don't leave. Give me a chance."

She wanted to scream. She wanted to cry. He looked so sincere. He sounded so sincere. And she wanted so desperately to believe him. But he was putting on the biggest act in the history of outdoor theater.

"You haven't asked me what I'm going to do with Paradise Springs," she said.

He shook his head. He didn't even look interested.

"I'm selling it to you." He didn't speak. "If you still want it." If he still wanted it. That was *all* he wanted.

"Why?"

"For all the reasons you gave me the first day I arrived. I'm afraid of heights, you're not. I don't ride. You do. I'm a city person. You're not."

"I don't want the land," he said.

She couldn't help laughing. A mirthless laugh. "I don't, either," she said.

"Are you saying you don't feel anything for me?" he asked, as if he hadn't heard her.

"Of course I do. I feel grateful for all the help you've given me. All the good advice." She clenched her hands into tight fists, digging her nails into her palms. Just a few more minutes and she'd be out of there. Away from him and his lies. Love, marriage. What did he take her for? A complete idiot?

"I'm afraid I just don't feel the same way you do, Zeb," she said willing her voice to stay even. "It must be a shock to be turned down, after all those other women falling all over you. But we're too different, you and I. It could never work."

"Okay, we're different. But that doesn't mean we can't work around our differences. Enjoy our differences." He finally dropped his arms and began to pace back and forth. "I don't get it. This doesn't make sense. You called your hospital. What did they say to make you change your mind?''

Chloe hadn't intended to bring up her ex-husband, but Zeb was proving more tenacious than she'd imagined. She thought he'd give up easier. Especially after he knew he could have the land.

''If you must know…''

''I must,'' he said grimly.

''I heard that my ex-husband has broken up with his girlfriend. That he misses me. I realize that I, uh…I miss him too.''

''Did you miss him the night we made love in the hot tub?'' he demanded, his eyes boring holes in her. ''Did you miss him that day we had a picnic in the meadow?''

''No, of course not,'' she said, proud of how matter-of-fact she sounded when her heart was beating like a tom-tom. ''But as you said, it was just a summer romance. Let's leave it at that.''

''Let's not,'' he said.

Alarmed by the fierce look in his eyes, she turned to go, but he grabbed her by the wrist.

She pushed against his shoulder with her free hand, afraid of the sparks igniting between them once again. He bent over and took her mouth in one desperate movement, crushing her lips with his, branding her forever with his mark. She could go back to San Francisco, she could go to Timbuktu, but she knew she'd never forget this kiss.

If only he'd let it go at that. One kiss. A farewell kiss. But he didn't. He deepened the kiss. Drugging her, filling her with such desperate longing that she responded as she'd never done before. Kissing him in return, with helpless abandon, with frustration, with pain and pleasure, knowing it would be their last embrace. Unable to resist, she gave in to the passion and the power of his kisses. While one hand tangled in her hair, the other slid down her hips and pulled her close, until she felt the heat of his arousal.

The power of the man thrilled her, excited her and scared her. She'd almost sacrificed her independence and her career to stay here with him. Just to watch him take over her property—for the money. Only the money. And still she wanted him. She could deny it from here to kingdom come, but deep down she knew the truth. She loved him and she always would, God help her.

Even knowing what she knew. Even knowing that he'd played her for a fool. That even now, after handing over the land, he continued to lie to her.

She moaned deep in her throat. Then, with every ounce of strength left in her body, she shoved him away, turned and ran. Ran for her life, for her sanity and for her future.

Zeb stood staring after Chloe for a long time, long after she'd disappeared around the corner of the barn. So long he half expected the calf he'd been observing for signs of foot-and-mouth disease would have grown up by the time he turned around. But it hadn't. It was still gamboling around the corral with the other calves. The sun was still high in the sky. Fleecy masses of clouds still floated in the upper air.

Everything was the same. Except him.

He was drained. Hollow. He leaned against the fence so he wouldn't fall down. He felt nothing.

Nothing but emptiness. She was gone. She didn't love him. She'd just left him for somebody else. So what else was new? It was his brother who'd told him he should take a chance, a second chance on love.

It was his brother who found him there still leaning against the fence as the sun sank behind the mountains in the distance. Still staring off toward Paradise Springs. In shock. In denial. In disbelief.

"What in the hell..." Sam said.

"She's gone," Zeb said. "Gone home."

"Didn't take the news well, then? About your lying to her?"

Zeb shook his head. "Didn't even get a chance to tell her." He laughed but he felt like crying. "She's selling us the land, though. Doesn't want it. Wants to go back to her ex. It's déjà vu all over again, Sam."

Sam put his arm around his brother's shoulder and they walked to the house. When they got to the kitchen through the back door, Sam shoved his brother into a chair and put the coffeepot on.

"Let's go over this again," Sam said.

"Spare me."

But Sam insisted. "She came over to say goodbye, right?"

Zeb nodded.

"Because she suddenly decided she was going to give up her dream of a spa and go back to her ex-husband?"

"Yes, I told you, yes."

"I don't get it."

"That's the way women are," Zeb said bitterly.

Still hearing Chloe's words echo in his head. *Summer romance. I miss him, too.*

"No they're not. Not Chloe. It doesn't make sense her bolting like that."

"Joanne did."

"Chloe isn't Joanne. She's different. She's real. She's in love with you. I swear I heard it in her voice, I saw it in her eyes."

Zeb glanced up at his brother. The poor guy was so serious, so intent on saving Zeb's feelings. It was really touching.

"It's okay," Zeb said. "I understand, even if you don't. I'm fine with it, really." He lifted his cup. "Thanks for the coffee. This is what I need. A shot of caffeine and I'll be okay. She just caught me off guard, that's all."

Sam looked dubious. If only Zeb could convince him, but first he had to convince himself.

"What if she found out," Sam said, pulling up a chair to sit across from Zeb. "About the dam, I mean."

"She didn't. I told you I didn't get a chance to tell her."

"I mean from someone else," Sam suggested.

"She hasn't been anywhere else except with us," Zeb said. "We made sure of that. Who would have told her?"

"Anyone. Wilma, Barney, Archie."

"Uh-uh. I would have known. You don't know her. She would have been furious. Exploded. She wasn't. She was calm. In control. I made a complete ass of myself. Telling her I loved her." He buried his head in his hands.

Sam jumped to his feet. "I'm going over there and find out what this is all about."

"No, you're not."

"Then you go," Sam said.

"What, so I can hear it all over again? How she doesn't feel anything for me except gratitude, how she doesn't belong here, that all she wanted was a summer romance...I've had enough for one day. I'll go tomorrow," he said, just to pacify his brother.

He had no intention of ever setting foot on Paradise Springs again. He could never soak in that tub again without thinking of her, without remembering how she floated above him, her breasts only inches away from his lips, teasing and tantalizing him to the brink of no return. He didn't want to drink from her mineral springs or ride his horse through her orchard, either. Not tomorrow. Not ever.

"She might be gone by tomorrow," Sam said.

"I know."

She was gone the next day. Despite himself, Zeb rode over, drawn there like a magnet, half hoping, half dreading she'd still be there. But she wasn't. Some of her things were still there. Her hammock swung in the breeze between two trees. Her tin cup and plate were on a rock next to her campsite. Otherwise the place was deserted. Water dripped listlessly into the pool, the bathhouse leaned forlornly to one side.

Zeb opened the door to her cabin, the one she'd cleaned so vigorously. Canned goods were stacked on the floor. Her portable espresso maker next to the bed. Too heavy to carry out. But her inflatable mattress was gone. Zeb bent over to pick up a crumpled newspaper from the floor. The headline leapt out at him. Flooding Persists. New Hope for Proponents of Dam Site.

His chest tightened. The air rushed out of his lungs, leaving him gasping for air. Sam was right. She knew. And she never said anything. Why not? Why hadn't she let him have it, right between the eyes, the way he deserved? Because she was proud. And she was hurt. He'd lied to her, he'd tricked her and she knew it. All the time she knew it.

He sat on the cabin floor and read the article, putting himself in her shoes, learning that she'd been betrayed. And worse, thinking he'd come on to her to get her land away from her. He couldn't deny the first part, he had no excuse for not telling her about the dam, for trying to cheat her out of the money. It was greed, pure and simple. But he couldn't let her go on thinking he'd made love to her with ulterior motives. He couldn't and he wouldn't. He'd find her and tell her and then let her go back to her ex-husband.

She'd be somewhere on Highway 40 heading west, but he had no idea how he'd find her. She had a day's head start on him. He got onto his horse, went back to the ranch, told Sam, who packed his bag for him, and got into his car.

It took him twelve hours of driving to find her. He couldn't go too fast for fear of missing her. He couldn't go too slow for fear of losing her. By some miracle—maybe old Horatio was guiding him—he pulled off at a truck stop in a small town in Utah and saw her car parked in front of the motel.

He checked in and reserved the room next to hers.

Then he walked across the parking lot and peered in the window of the restaurant. She was sitting alone in a booth with a plate of meat loaf and mashed potatoes in front of her. His heart pounded. His throat was so dry he was afraid he wouldn't be able to speak after coming all this way. He might have to scribble something on a napkin. What would it be— I'm Sorry or I Love You? No, she'd just rip it up.

Instead he walked past the hostess and sat down across from Chloe. In desperation he took a large gulp from the glass of beer in front of her. If he hadn't he'd have been speechless. "I thought you didn't drink beer," he said. Good work, he told himself. Travel hundreds of miles, rehearse what you're going to say and then blow it.

Calmly, she pushed the glass across the table. "I don't. I ordered it for you. I saw you coming across the parking lot." She sighed loudly as if he'd interrupted something important. "What do you want, Zeb, besides the beer? Where are you going?"

"Going?" he asked, leaning back against the booth and drinking her in like a thirsty man in the desert. Ignoring the noisy truckers at the next table, he said, "Going here, wherever this is. Going wherever you are."

"Why?"

"I have something to say. Something I didn't say the last time I saw you. It won't take long. And then in the morning I'll leave. Go back home. Go ahead, finish your meat loaf."

"That's okay. I'm not that hungry. Maybe I'll have a glass of white wine."

"In Utah?" he asked, determined to get her whatever she wanted if he had to drive all the way to California to get it. But when he signaled the waiter, he nodded understandingly and in minutes was back with an icy-cold glass of something that at least looked like white wine.

She looked at him over her glass, perfectly still, huge dark eyes in a pale oval face, watching, waiting for him to say something.

He took another drink of the pale amber liquid before he began, gripping the glass so his hands wouldn't shake, more nervous than he'd ever been in his life. Even more so than the time when he'd risked his life in an amateur rodeo.

"You knew, didn't you, about the dam?" he said. She nodded.

"You knew I wanted to buy your land and resell it and make money off it. I'm sorry. Really sorry for lying to you. Withholding the truth, whatever. It was despicable."

Her lower lip trembled. "Not as despicable as making love to me. Was that really necessary?" she asked, blinking back a tear.

He wanted to reach across the table and brush her tears away. He wanted to hold her and make the pain disappear. But he only braced his elbows on the table and leaned forward. "Listen to me, Chloe. Making love to you had nothing to do with your land."

"It was effective, though," she said. "I almost believed that you cared about me."

"I did. I do."

"Yes. Sure. Well, if that's all..."

He put his hand on her arm. "No, that's not all. I

don't know how this happened, but somewhere along
the way, I fell in love with you.''

She pulled away from him. ''Yes, that's what you
said yesterday.''

''You didn't believe me,'' he said. It wasn't a
question. He knew she didn't.

''Why should I?'' she asked, shifting in her seat.

''Because it's true.'' He was getting desperate. She
was getting restless. What if she got up and left?
What could he do to keep her there? To make her
listen to him? Why *should* she believe him? ''Chloe,
what if you sold the land to the Bureau of Reclamation and used the money to build your spa somewhere else?''

''Where?''

''At the Bar Z.''

''A spa at your ranch? You laughed at the idea,
remember?'' she said.

''Because of the long hike in and the lack of facilities. Bar Z has a road and electricity.''

''You said I needed a whole lot of money,'' she
reminded him.

''You'll have a whole lot of money.''

''You called it a 'fat farm',' she said.

''I'm sorry.''

''What about you and your cows?''

''There ought to be room for everybody, me and
Sam and the cattle and you and your fa…your family,'' he said.

''What's in it for you?'' she asked, taking a sip of
her wine.

''You. You're in it for me. I'd get to see you from
time to time.''

She surveyed him through narrowed eyes. "What else?"

"Rent money."

"So it would be a business deal," she said, tapping her finger against her glass.

"If that's what you want," he said, unable to keep from hoping, from praying that maybe she was seriously considering what he'd been thinking about for the last twelve hours.

"What do *you* want?" she asked.

"What do I want?" Was it his imagination or was her tone a little softer, were her eyes a little brighter? "I told you yesterday I wanted to marry you. I still want to marry you. But I know that's not what you want. You want a summer romance, and marriage tends to go on all year. You said you'd go crazy in the winter up there, so..."

"Shut up," she said, the tears brimming over and running down her cheeks. "Just shut up. I'm tired of hearing what you think I want. You don't know anything about what I want." With that she jumped to her feet and rushed out of the restaurant.

He watched her run across the parking lot to the motel and slam the door of her room after her. She was running, but not too far. He drained his glass, paid the bill, went outside and took his bag out of his car before going to his room. The room next to hers. He plugged in his electric toothbrush, his shaver and another appliance he'd brought along.

He put his ear against the wall and heard her crying. He forced himself to stay where he was. This time she had to come to him. But what if she didn't? She had to. He called the front desk and complained she was making too much noise. Two minutes later there was a knock on the door. He heaved a sigh of relief.

She was wearing shorts and a sweatshirt. Her hands were on her hips. Her cheeks were streaked, her hair was tangled, her eyes were almost black. She was glaring at him, and her chin was tilted at a very stubborn angle. He thought she'd never looked more beautiful.

"How dare you call and complain about me?" Chloe demanded. "How dare you rent the room next to mine, anyway?"

"It's a good location, next to the ice machine. But I can't sleep with all that noise," he said. "Come in and have a nightcap."

She peered around him and sniffed the air. "It smells like coffee." After a long day on the road, it smelled like heaven.

"Espresso. I brought your coffeemaker back to you. You forgot it."

"You're pretty confident. What if you hadn't found me?" she asked, stepping cautiously into the room. "How far would you have gone?"

"To the moon," he said.

"That's not necessary," she said, studying his craggy face, creased with new lines of fatigue and worry, as if she'd never seen it before. Just an hour ago she had thought she'd never see it again. Just an hour ago she'd been sure she'd never cry again—not after sobbing her way through most of Colorado. Then he showed up, and the tears flowed once again. Tears of relief, indecision and a tiny ray of hope.

"Sit down, I'll pour the coffee," he said.

She sat on the edge of the king-size bed and watched him pour dark, rich espresso into two paper cups.

"I've been thinking about your offer," she said. "It's very generous in view of what you'd hoped for, you know, the whole...thing."

He shrugged as if it didn't matter, but she knew it did.

"What bothers me is not carrying on the family tradition, not fulfilling my great-grandfather's dream of making a go of the springs."

"Are you sure that was his dream?" he asked, as he handed her the coffee and casually sank down next to her on the bed. "With Horatio it was easy come, easy go. I think he won Paradise Springs in a poker game. He didn't attach that much importance to a piece of land. He once said it was just a place to hang his hat. He was very adaptable."

"That's what Mr. Crane said," she said.

"You went to see Archie...oh, God, Chloe, you don't think..."

"What else could I think? You did everything to keep me from talking to him. You even took me on a picnic and made love to me." She was still indignant, but it was getting harder and harder to stay angry. The warmth of the coffee, the heat of his body next to hers, the memory of that magic afternoon were slowly melting the hard core of resentment she'd built up inside her.

"Making love to you had nothing to do with taking your land," he said. "For the record, I didn't mean to fall in love with you. I didn't mean to fall in love with anyone. It's so damned inconvenient.

Here I am, miles away from home, making a fool of myself, while you—'' He ran his hand through his hair and glanced at her, ''What are you smiling at?''

She put one hand on his shoulder and smiled up at him through her tears. ''I can't help it. I didn't want to fall in love with you, either. I didn't want a summer romance, or any kind of romance. Talk about inconvenient. I don't know what to do.'' She bit her lip and looked at him for the answer.

But he didn't give her one. He wasn't going to make it easy for her.

He tucked a strand of her hair behind her ear and she shivered at his touch. Wanting more. So much more.

''Maybe we ought to think this over,'' he said. ''Sleep on it.''

''Fine,'' she said, setting her coffee on the bedside table. ''As long as we sleep on it together.''

He nodded, a very relieved smile spreading across his face. He snapped off the light and then slowly, slowly, with the most infinite care slid her shirt off over her shoulders, removed her bra, buried his head between her breasts and breathed her name.

Every ounce of her resistance was gone, melted in the heat of his embrace. Still she wanted more. Kneeling on the mattress, she unbuttoned his shirt, then his jeans and threw them in a heap on the floor. He might not be in a hurry, but she was. He might be willing to think it over. She wasn't. She'd been thinking for the past two days and she wanted to stop thinking and feel. Feel him on top of her, inside her and all around her.

She wasn't disappointed. He made love to her with

everything he had to offer, heart, soul and body. Her last doubts vanished sometime before dawn.

Just one thing bothered her. Just one question remained. As the light from passing truckers' headlights filtered through the curtains, she paused and traced his rough jawline with her fingers, loving the touch of him, loving the look of him. Even the way his hair stood on end in ten directions, the way his eyelids drooped at half-mast.

"How are we going to sleep on it, if we never sleep?" she asked.

"May have to stay another night," he said. "But I'm not sure that would do it. There's something about you and a bed, or a tub...or a garden. There's something about you that keeps me from sleeping."

"You can sleep when you get home."

He rolled over on his side and propped his head in his hand. "Not going home, unless you go with me."

"What would you do, follow me all the way to San Francisco?"

"To the moon."

She smiled, rolled out of bed and began dressing. "We'd better get going, then."

"To the moon?" he asked, sitting on the edge of the bed to watch her pull her shorts up her long, gorgeous legs.

"To the ranch. To the Bar Z. Home."

Epilogue

The snow drifted halfway to the eaves of the ranch house that winter. Fence posts were buried. Most of the livestock huddled in the barn. The new bull had his own quarters befitting his stature. Sam Bowie was in Denver taking a class in animal husbandry. The other two Bowies, the newlyweds, sat by the fire in the evenings, drinking cappuccino made in a large new machine that had been a Christmas present from Zeb to Chloe, reminiscing about old times and planning for the future.

Chloe handed Zeb the copy for her brochure. "What do you think of this?" she asked.

Paradise Hot Springs, where the Ute Indians once wintered near warm thermal waters, has relocated upstream to the Bar Z Ranch. Through the miracle of modern technology, the same mineral waters known to cure gout, obesity, broken hearts and old gunshot wounds will still be available to today's spa guests, as well as massages, horseback riding and gourmet meals. Guests will be met by horse-drawn coach or van. El. 8000 ft. Your genial hostess and proprietor: Chloe Hudson Bowie.

"You've got me hooked. I'd come. Just to see the genial hostess meet me by horse-drawn coach," he said.

"You think I couldn't do it?" she asked standing in front of the hearth with her hands on her hips. "Just because I can't ride a horse doesn't mean I can't drive a team, does it?"

"Sweetheart, you can do anything you put your mind to," he said, pulling her into his lap. He lifted the curls off the back of her neck to kiss her soft skin and inhale her intoxicating scent. "Who else could convert half a cattle ranch into a luxury spa?"

She snuggled into his arms. "Not quite yet. But I couldn't have even made a start on this project without you. You're the one who rerouted the stream, who dug into the side of the hill to find your own spring."

"*Our* own spring," he reminded her.

"Our own spring. Our own ranch and our own bull and our own Jacuzzi.

Which reminds me," she added. "One of the great pleasures of winter is soaking in our new tub and watching the snow fall outside the window."

"One of my great pleasures is sharing that tub